Also by Carole Walker Carter

The Child Rowanda

Return to Arolsen

Carole Walker Carter

The Child Rowanda Series

Volume 2

WALKER CARTER PUBLISHING, LLC

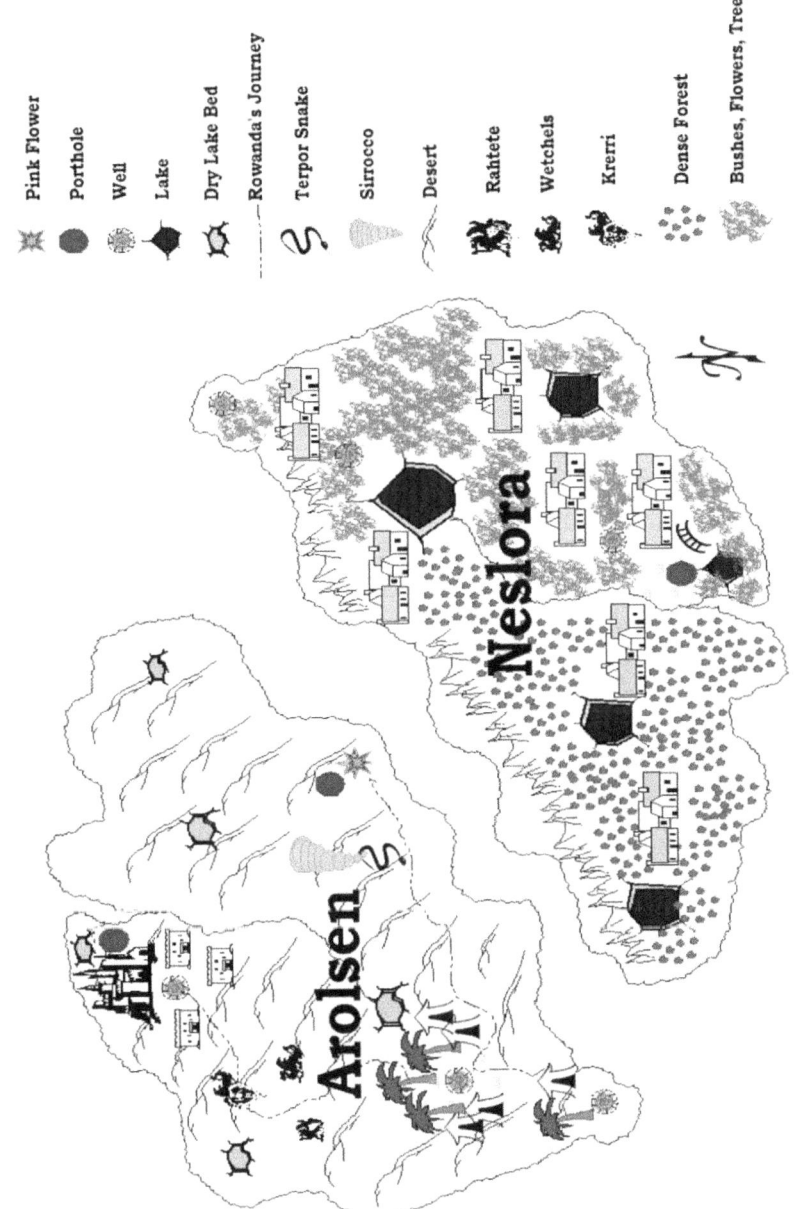

	Pink Flower
	Porthole
	Well
	Lake
	Dry Lake Bed
	Rowanda's Journey
	Terpor Snake
	Sirocco
	Desert
	Rahtete
	Wetcheis
	Krerri
	Dense Forest
	Bushes, Flowers, Trees

Neslora

Arolsen

Cover Design and Layout by Donald E Carter
Cover Photos © Fotolia by Adobe

The Child Rowanda, Return to Arolsen / by Carole Walker Carter

The Child Rowanda Series / Volume 2

ISBN 978-1-947734-48-7

9 8 7 6 5 4 3 2 1 17 18 19 20 21

[1. Swords, 2. Sorcery, 3. Magical Charms,
4. Action & Adventure, 5. Wands, 6. Underworld, 7. Talisman, 8. Demons,
9. Spirits, 10. Magical Creatures]

WALKER CARTER PUBLISHING, LLC

Please check out my website at www.walkercarter.com

To my girls Jennifer and Lisa, my grandson Nixon, my granddaughter Alex and my husband, Don.

In memory of my mother and dad, Elda and Dean Walker.

I will always love you!!!

ACKNOWLEDGMENTS

I wrote this book in cooperation with my best friend and husband, Donald E. Carter, author of _Concurrent Engineering, Product Development Environment_ business books. Don's inspiration and support helped me to create characters for The Child Rowanda Series. Don researched all the technical information.

The first book in The Child Rowanda Series is _Little Dragon_. The second book in the series is _Return to Arolsen_. The third book in the series is _Underworld_. The fourth book in the series is _Dragon Princess_.

Janis Lane supported me with my writing by cheering me on to tell my stories. Don and I worked diligently to edit this book over the past year.

My girls, Jennifer and Lisa Coyle, provided several useful resource books. Without their support and prodding, this book may still be in draft form. Jennifer, with a keen eye for graphics, helped Don with the cover art.

Without my older sister, Linda Sturgill, and younger sister Janel Walker, giving me love, support, and resources, I would not be able to write. They each spent hours proofreading and editing the _Aztarian Series_ Books and _Evers & MacFarlan Detective Series_ Books. I will forever be grateful for my family's encouragement and dedication to my creations.

Special Thanks to all those that donated to my GoFundMe page, Linda Sturgill, Elda Walker, Janel Walker, Judy Mathiesen, Linda Maddex, Afsaneh Fowler, and Carol Royce Davidson. These donations kick-started my venture by allowing me to acquire editing tools, printed proof copies, ISBN numbers, audio equipment, and final publication costs.

TABLE OF CONTENTS

CHAPTER ONE

*Father* was such a strange word to be calling Beir, but now that he was no longer a fugitive slave on Arolsen, Beirimor's demeanor had softened, and it was easier to talk with him. Rowanda and her mother would sit and listen to her father's experiences in the desert of Arolsen for hours. Rowanda's mother listened in horror when Rowanda would tell of her own adventures with wetchels and terpor.

"Remember when you tried to start a dust-devil, and it spun you up into the air, and you couldn't get down?" laughed Beir. "You should have seen her spinning around and around up in the swirling wind, Graciella."

Rowanda joined in the laughter with her mother, still looking horrified at the mental picture of her daughter caught up in a small tornado. Seeing the tears running down both husband's and daughter's cheeks from laughing so hard, Graciella decided Rowanda must not have been in too much danger, or they would not find it so funny.

"What is a terpor?" asked Rowanda's mother.

Rowanda, still laughing with her father, replied, "It is an enormous serpent that one wants to avoid in the desert."

"And you truly fought one?" Graciella's eyes widened in shock at the thought that her daughter had been in such danger.

"Relax, Graciella. She is home safe. She was amazing, though. You should have seen her in action. On second thought, it is a good thing you didn't see her. You would have fainted," Beir said as he gathered his wife into his arms for a hug.

Indignant, Graciella pushed away from her husband's embrace. "I would not have fainted. I am tougher than you think, or I would not have survived as a slave at the palace for as long as I did!"

Pulling Graciella into his arms once again, the mood now serious, Beir said, "I know how rough it was to be a slave. Remember, I was one for many years and not just a week."

"Now, you are trying to make me feel guilty," Graciella said.

"Just the opposite. I just wanted you to know that I, too, know exactly what you endured. You must have been strong to endure the hardships of being a slave."

Feeling bad for both of her parents, Rowanda added, "Mother, I came as soon as I could, honestly."

"Oh, Sweetie, I didn't mean to make you feel bad. You were amazing. You are my hero. I would still be there, and so would your father if it were not for you," Graciella said contritely.

A knock at the door interrupted the family. Rushing to the door, Rowanda opened it to find her best friend, Nalivia, standing on the threshold with a broad grin on her face.

Nalivia, a short, freckled-faced, redheaded girl, grabbed Rowanda, and the two jumped up and down in delight at seeing each other again. "Can I go outside with Nalivia?" Rowanda asked in excitement.

"Go…and have some fun. You deserve it," Graciella said with a smile of relief on her face. It was good to see her daughter acting like a child again.

Once outside, the two girls ran off, giggling. Finding their favorite spot in the garden, they collapsed into the soft grass and chatted away like magpies.

"First off, thank you so much for saving my mother. Secondly, how did you do it?" Nalivia asked.

Rowanda settled back into the grass and stared up into the branches of the tree she had climbed so often. "Well, it wasn't easy, but I did have my father and Boultori to help me. With the charms, Grandmother Emeraza gave to me, I had a fighting chance."

Rowanda stopped talking for a few moments and then added, "It is so odd to have a father after all these years thinking he was dead. And to find out that Emeraza, our Elder, is my grandmother is kinda spooky. I really don't know how to act towards her. It isn't like she is sweet and cuddly as my grandmother Salitha. Can you imagine rushing into Emeraza's arms for a big hug?"

"No way! She scares me to death!" Nalivia laughed. "You still haven't told me how you rescued our mothers."

Rowanda gathered her thoughts. "I want to make the story short as I can so as not to bore you too much. Basically, I created a wind storm to keep the prison guards away, and then I opened a confluence, and we all stepped through back to Neslora."

"You sure made it sound easy. Do you think someday I will be able to do what you did?" Nalivia asked with eagerness in her voice.

"I would suspect Emeraza will have no choice but to start our training soon. Even though we are young, we have the gift of sorcery, and the Elder would not want us to experiment on our own," Rowanda replied.

Letting all seriousness leave their discussions, the two girls talked like the schoolgirls they were. Rowanda mentioned a particular young man from Arolsen that caught her eye. "Nalivia, he was so cute. His name is Anarigar. I often thought I would like to bring him here," giggled Rowanda.

"You are so bad, Rowanda. If you brought him here, I might have given you a run for your money. You know we don't have many cute boys in our village," Nalivia remarked.

"What about Garus? I see you watching him all the time," chuckled Rowanda.

Nalivia blushed and changed the subject. "What is a desert-like anyway?"

"Just awful...it is hot, dry, and has almost no plants at all. Not only that, but there are terpors, wetchels and krerri chasing you all the time. The nomads want to capture you and sell you as a slave, and the king is mean. I wouldn't want to go back there...except to see Boultori and Anarigar again."

Shocked, Nalivia remarked, "No plants! I can't imagine a world that is not lush, green, and full of lovely plants. You mean there is no grass to walk on or lie down upon? There are no flowers or trees or anything?"

"I only saw a few trees and grass at the oasis. Other than that, there was nothing to be seen but sand in every direction one looked. The lack of water is one reason the terpor and wetchels were always hunting us. They didn't want to eat us for food. They wanted our body's water content. We wore cloaks that covered us from head to foot so the creatures could not smell our perspiration. It was really, truly awful!" Rowanda exclaimed.

"If there was no water or plants, what did you eat while you were there?" asked Nalivia curiously.

"Oh, we did have some dates from the trees around the oasis. The dates were a treat. Otherwise, we ate lizards and stuff like that. Truly, it was not as bad tasting as one would think," Rowanda told her best friend.

"Lizards! You really ate lizards?" screeched Nalivia.

"Yes, and lizard eggs as well. One will eat most anything when one is hungry. Just hope you never find yourself in the same situation," Rowanda added.

"I would die before I ate a lizard!" announced Nalivia.

"Yeah, right!" Rowanda countered.

Leaving the talk of the desert behind, the girls got up and chased around the garden, playing hide and seek and any silly game that came to their minds. Rowanda was ecstatic to just be able to relax and be mindless after her experiences in the desert. All she wanted to do was forget about Arolsen.

CHAPTER TWO

The elders and the mothers met in the town hall to discuss whether the girls were old enough to begin formal training as apprentice sorceresses. The debate in the room continued for hours. Finally, Emeraza hushed the group and said, "If Rowanda did not possess a strong, innate ability, many of you in this room would still be slaves. I don't think we can retake the chance. We need to train our young girls now before we have another situation. Someone from Arolsen possesses the ability and knowledge to open a confluence. We never know when more of our people will be abducted for some evil purpose. We must be prepared and ready. All of us older sorceresses are becoming weak in our powers. We are no longer able to protect our community. It is time for the younger girls to step up and take our places."

None of the Elders wanted to hear the truth, but they admitted what Emeraza said was true. With a vote of hands, it was decided the girls would start formal training at the beginning of the next moon. In the meantime, much was needed of the elders including finding enough charms for the incoming group of young sorceresses. That in itself would take the weeks remaining before the new moon.

The meeting was ended with each elder knowing exactly what she must do. Emeraza felt saddened that the young girls' lives, as they now knew it, would come to an end. Having to grow up so quickly had been hard for Emeraza. She knew it would be hard for the young girls to leave their childhood behind. Having the responsibility to protect all of Neslora laid at their feet was difficult at such a tender age.

Salitha lingered behind to talk with Emeraza. She, too, had concerns about how much responsibilities were being put upon the children. Stopping Emeraza at the door, she said, "I had a dream last night."

Emeraza knew immediately it was not an ordinary dream. Salitha was gifted with the ability to see into the future. She hesitated to ask Salitha about her dream. Rarely were Salitha's dreams a good sign of things to come. She had foreseen the abduction of citizens for decades but was not able to see the exact time or place, so there was little to do to stop the abductions.

"What did you dream, Salitha?" Emeraza finally asked.

"My dream was silent. No birds were singing happily in the trees. The bees were no longer merrily flying about from flower to flower. Our world was devoid of plants and water." Salitha paused for effect. "I also saw two new confluences opening and many men coming through to capture our citizens…. This time, I know where the two new confluences will appear. I just don't know when."

Emeraza stood still. She was thoughtful for a while, and then she said, "Is this dream a warning of things that will come true or can we do something to stop it?"

Salitha sighed. "My dreams are never without change. Occurrences can happen to affect the outcome. I feel we can make preparations to do so right now. Unfortunately, our training of the girls will need to be rushed. I feel the girls may be instrumental in the outcome. Our world as we know it will change…and not for the better, if we fail to train the new apprentice sorceresses successfully and quickly."

"All the more reason to find charms without haste. Each girl will need four. That means we must have almost double the number to make sure the girls have choices. I remember I had over twenty-five talismans laid on the table for Rowanda to make her choice. Luckily, four of them selected her. We must hurry. Our instructions will entail long days with few breaks to fit into the short time span we have. I fear the girls' attention at this age may wander. I can be strict, but I will need you to be as well. I know it is not in your nature, but our world may depend on it. Can you stop being a grandmother and become a disciplinarian?" Emeraza asked, peering over her half-glasses, she focused intensely deep into Salitha's eyes.

"I guess I will become what I need to become. If I fail, there is always a potion I can concoct," said Salitha with a wink.

Emeraza chuckled, knowing precisely what Salitha would mix together to make her the old witch she was referencing. "I hope you will not need to go to that extreme."

The next day, most of the elder sorceresses went out upon the land in search of the many talisman and charms needed to start the education and training of the young sorceresses. The charms would be found in places all over the land and in unexpected places as well. Each elder sorceress carried a large burlap bag in which to place the charms and an overnight bag with personal items. Villages along their routes would gladly take the women in for the nights they traveled. The residents of Neslora knew how instrumental the Elders were in their existence and their very way of life.

Rural dwellers' livestock grazed on lush fields of grass while their crops grew in fertile soil. All the inhabitants of Neslora knew this was not always true. Life had been a struggle for most of the people before the sorceresses of old had discovered their talents and applied them to air, water, soil, and fire. The results were staggering, and Neslorians appreciated the lifestyle that followed.

The sorceresses were never called witches or necromancers—terms often offensive to the women. No black magic was ever practiced. All magic in Neslora benefited the residents of the country, and the people admired the women greatly.

As the new moon approached, the elders began to return back to their village. Each one displayed the multiple charms they had found and placed them upon the expanded table in the town hall, which would serve as the training center from the new moon until completion of the training.

The few sorceresses, too old to travel, remained home to gather herbs and other materials necessary to teach enchantments and healing arts. These items were also collected and brought to the town hall for future classes. Once all the elders returned from their search, and all the charms were set on the table, the girls would be gathered, and each would be challenged, one at a time, to find the charms that accepted them.

Alfinia returned from the south with a horrible story to relay to Emeraza and the gathered elders. She stood at the front of the assembly and told what she discovered. "While in the furthest point of our land, I came upon a property that was deserted. The land was barren, and the family farming the territory had left to work in the nearby village. I went to the village and found the family who explained that suddenly, the plants started to dry up and wither away. There was no longer grass for the livestock or food growing in their gardens, so they had no choice but to leave."

"Did you ask when this started?" Emeraza questioned.

"Yes, Elder, I did ask, and they said it happened just over a moon ago. The head of the family said all was good one day, and the next, it was devastation," Alfinia replied.

"Then it was not disease or pestilence. It was black magic! Who would have done such a thing to our beautiful country? I know it was not one of us," Emeraza stated. "We will discuss this further once the girls have gone home to eat and sleep, but for now, we will table the discussion as I see the girls coming in this direction."

The elders, all sorceresses, expressing worry and concern, nodded their heads in agreement and gathered at the door to greet the young girls who would soon become one of their order. Forcing smiles on their faces, all traces of the previous conversation was hidden behind the kind, familiar faces the girls knew as grandmothers.

The village Rowanda and her playmates had grown up in was a unique town. Only the family members of the sorceresses lived in it. This village was intentionally sheltered and protected by enchantments to raise the next group of sorceresses, knowing it skipped a generation. The daughters of the elders knew they may be carrying the future hope for their land. The fathers, a son of an Elder sorceress, also knew their responsibility. They protected their women and families fiercely, but also provided food and shelter.

Rowanda had never known her father growing up. Thinking him dead, she never thought to ask many questions. It was not until she met the stern, determined man known as Beir, that she ever thought about the training the young men from her village endured. Every one of them was a warrior, even though there was no enemy to fight. It was understood from the beginning that the sorceresses were not fragile beings that had no defense, but they needed protection if they were ever invaded. It would seem the men's defensive training might be required soon. The men of their village were more than capable of meeting most any attack.

Rowanda had a fleeting thought of the men of their village as she entered the town hall. Her mind was now focused on what she might need to learn. Being the only girl in the village who actually ever used charms, she also knew how much she did not really know. Her experiences on Arolsen only intensified her need to learn as much as possible. Rowanda was aware she barely escaped many the dangers on Arolsen by chance and not by skill or knowledge. Having an innate ability served her well, but she also knew it could have failed her at any moment while struggling to survive in the desert. In fact, the one failure, though hysterical at the time, could have ended badly for her if she had not dropped from the dust devil with only the wind knocked out of her lungs.

"Good morning, Rowanda," came the greeting from the various elders as she entered the room with the other six girls behind her. The greetings continued with "Good morning, Magdelan. Good morning, Estelle. Good morning, Breanna. Good morning, Opaline. Good morning, Nalivia. Good morning, Thaliana. Please take a seat at the front of the hall."

The girls each found a seat and settled themselves into the chairs, knowing it would be a long day with only short breaks. The elders made sure the chairs were not too comfortable for fear the girls might fall asleep. Not all of the studies would be exciting. Some knowledge passed to the next group of sorceresses would be annoying to them, but essential nonetheless.

At first, it was as dull as the girls feared with history lessons. The elders felt that knowing the past could facilitate the future. Some of the history lessons were the lives of the present elders, and each enjoyed telling their own story in detail, much to the chagrin of the girls gathered. Yawning started, and soon the elders' sterner demeanor began to appear.

"Sit up straight and close your mouth," barked one elder to her own granddaughter as the girl stifled a yawn.

"We know that much of what you hear this morning is not exciting to you. There is a reason why you must hear the stories and absorb them. Each has valuable lessons for you, and the subtle lessons you will learn will serve you well. You must open your minds and receive each story as a gift of love from your elders. One day, it will be you standing in our positions reliving your stories. We deserve your respect and undivided attention. We will take a short break so that you can return more focused. Be back in ten minutes," Emeraza scolded.

The girls quickly but silently filed out the door. Once outside, they ran and played with the joy of their young years. The elders knew only too well how long the training would seem to the exuberant fledglings.

"I think that went well," Scherra said to the other elders as they watched the girls playing. "I wish we had more time to take the training slower. They are so young yet. We did not start our education until we were sixteen years old. Four years makes a big difference with attention span."

Emeraza just shook her head. "It is what it is. We can't delay what we know and what is happening."

The elders each went to their stations and prepared for the upcoming lessons of the day. Knowing the girl's interest would be sparked if each would receive their personal charms, Emeraza decided to allow this lesson to happen out of the usual sequence of the teaching order. Moving the talismans around the table, giving space for each, Emeraza was ready for the students to return.

As the girls once more arrived, feeling refreshed from play, Emeraza asked them to spread out around the large table in the front of the hall. "Don't touch anything on the table," barked Emeraza.

The girls immediately put their arms to their side and stood quietly in the presence of the elders and the odd assortment of gathered items. Stones, gems, branches, hand tools, weapons, feathers, claws, pottery, metalwork, pendants, pouches, and many other odd and familiar objects lay in view.

"Each of you will be guided, one at a time, to find your own personal talismans or charms if you would rather use that word. Know that each will pick you and not the other way around. When it is your turn to proceed with the selection, you will be asked to close your eyes, let your hand or hands float above the table and wait until you feel an object demanding your action. You may feel a hot sensation, cold sensation, a pull upon your hand, or even a prickling or stinging sensation as if you are being stung by a wasp. Don't jerk your hand away but let me know immediately what you are feeling and I will direct you from that point.

"Magdelan, step forward, close your eyes, and let your arms extend across the table. Tell me if you feel anything as you move your hands in the air above the items on the table," Emeraza directed the first child.

Magdelan did as she was told. She slowly moved her hands above the items laid on the table until she felt a cold sensation. "I feel something cold, Elder."

"Good, I want you to let your right hand slowly descend until you are touching the item," Emeraza instructed.

Magdelan let her hand touch an item. "Grasp it in your hand and hand it to me without opening your eyes." Emeraza continued to direct Magdelan through the process.

Soon Magdelan had four objects that had chosen her. She was told to step back from the table and open her eyes.

"Here are the four items that picked you." Emeraza held out each object and handed them to Magdelan one at a time. The first object represents *Earth*," Emeraza continued as she placed a pinecone into Magdelan's hand. Next, she put a river rock into the waiting girl's palm and told her it represented *Water*. An eagle's feather represented *Air*, and the last item given to Magdelan was a flint indicating its use would be *Fire*.

Nalivia was next. She found herself jumping from foot to foot as if she was standing on hot sand with bare feet when she touched her first talisman. Without opening her eyes, she exclaimed it was so hot it was burning her feet. The other girls laughed out loud at what a silly sight Nalivia made but was silenced immediately by Emeraza's raised hand and a hard stare.

Nalivia continued her search for her remaining charms and found, not to her delight when her eyes were finally allowed to open, but a lump of coal, a hand trowel, and a bumblebee's wing.

"My charms are so common. I was hoping for a dagger or gems or something more glamorous," Nalivia said with disappointment. "I only have three charms. That is not fair, and she started to cry. Immediately, her tear formed into a crystal and fell into her hand."

"That is your forth charm, Nalivia. Your teardrop will represent *Water*," Emeraza said, ignoring Nalivia's outburst and proceeded on.

Each child went through a similar process, gathering objects that belonged to them and them alone. Emeraza asked Rowanda to share with the groups the charms that had chosen her one month ago.

Rowanda quickly took out her sword and wand, and gasps from the other girls were heard. There were only two.

"Rowanda! Where are the other two charms? You had a chalice and a pouch of seed before you went to Arolsen. Where are they now?" demanded Emeraza.

Rowanda shrinking from her grandmother's loud, accusing voice, said meekly, "I left them in Arolsen for Boultori to use to help his country to become lush like ours."

Emeraza shrieked, "You did what?"

Rowanda was too afraid to repeat what she had just said. Instead, she stood mutely in place.

"Girls, go get something to eat now!" Emeraza said dismissing the other girls. "Not you, Rowanda. You stay here!"

As the other girls scurried to get out of the building, Nalivia looked back in fear at Rowanda. There was nothing she could do to help or protect her best friend.

Once the other children were out of earshot, Emeraza lowered her voice and asked Rowanda for details. "Exactly when and how did this happen?"

Rowanda immediately knew she had done something very wrong, but at the time, she had no idea she was doing anything but good. "Elder, I thought I was helping some good people in a horrible situation. Their world is so stark and dreadful. I wanted them to have what we have," Rowanda cried.

"I need to know what you did and when, Child," Emeraza stated.

"When I opened the confluence so the mothers, Beir and I could leave the prison, I thought Boultori would come with us. He said he could not leave his people when they needed him most. As the hole started to close, I passed him my chalice and pouch so he could grow plants for his people. It never occurred to me that it was a bad thing to do," Rowanda tried to explain.

Iona was the next to speak. "So that is why part of our southern country has dried up and become a wasteland. It seems your friend, Boultori, is already using your chalice and pouch to create an oasis near the palace. I am assuming the palace city would correspond to the location that has started to become desert. Am I correct, Emeraza?"

Emeraza said she would check with Beirimor to be sure, but she suspected that was the case. "As best as I can surmise, when Rowanda's charms are used in Arolsen by someone other than her, it affects our land. As long as the chalice and pouch are being used there, our country will suffer ill effects. We have no choice but to retrieve them. Rowanda, I fear that means you must return to Arolsen...."

CHAPTER THREE

 Rowanda started to cry in earnest at hearing those words. She did not want to return to Arolsen...ever. Now, it was her own fault that would make it necessary to do so.

"Rowanda, calm yourself. I have not decided on the particulars of your return yet. You will not be going alone, but I can't tell you anything more yet. I need to talk to your parents. I also need to talk with the Elders to decide on the best course. Classes are ended for today. Return to your home and tell your parents to come to the town hall now," Emeraza said with a dismissal of her hand.

As Rowanda left in tears, Salitha said to Emeraza, "You could have been gentler to the girl. She had no idea she was doing something wrong. Remember, we did not instruct her before she was given a task way beyond her age and abilities. I think a hug would have served her well."

Emeraza knew Salitha was correct, but she did not have the time to be patient or understanding. Neslora's whole existence was at stake.

When Graciella and Beirimor entered the town hall meeting, there was a fire in Graciella's eyes. "How dare you cause my child to cry like that. What happened, Mother-Elder?"

Beir touched Graciella to calm his wife. He knew his mother was strict, but he also knew her as a loving mother. "Graciella, give my mother a chance to tell us what happened."

Indicating a place to sit around the smaller table where the other elder sorceresses waited, Rowanda's parents took a seat. "We have some distressing news. It seems the chalice and pouch that Rowanda gave to your friend, Boultori, has terrible consequences here in Neslora. A charm from this world cannot be used in another world by anyone but the owner without affecting Neslora. The chalice and pouch of seeds are being used in Arolsen. From what I surmise, when Boultori uses the seeds and chalice to cause plants to grow in the desert, it causes the land corresponding here in Neslora to die. If Boultori continues to use Rowanda's charms in Arolsen, Neslora will soon be a desert."

Beir sat shocked, and Graciella covered her mouth in dismay. "I had no idea what could possibly happen when Rowanda shoved her two charms into Boultori's hands before the confluence closed, or I would have told you immediately," Beir said in his defense.

"I did not believe Boultori could be successful as no other wizard can use a charm that gave itself to a sorceress. However, if given freely, as Rowanda did for Boultori, the charms are on loan and can be used. That is what I think has happened. It is imperative that we get those charms back. Unfortunately, that means Rowanda must return to Arolsen to retrieve her charms from Boultori. No one else can do it for her."

"No way!" Graciella shouted. "My child is not going back to Arolsen for any reason."

Beir patted his wife's hand. "She will not go alone. I will go along to protect her, Graciella."

"Yes, Beir, you will be going, but you won't be the only one going either. We, the Elders, have discussed this before your arrival. It has

31

been decided that I will go as well, and so will Nalivia," Emeraza announced.

"Nalivia! Why, Nalivia?" asked Beir. "She is as untrained as Rowanda, and she does not have the sorceress gene on both sides of her family as Rowanda does. Why would you think she would have the same innate abilities that Rowanda possesses?"

Emeraza continued with her reasoning. "When Nalivia was at the table to collect her talismans, it was obvious from the ones that selected her, that she, too, had innate abilities that would serve our needs on Arolsen."

"Would you mind explaining a bit further?" asked Beir.

Emeraza continued, "Nalivia's charms are an unusual assortment. Coal, a trowel, a bumblebee's wing, and one unique charm that her own body produced, a crystalized teardrop. That has never happened before, and I don't know how it fits in, but I feel it is important. With that odd combination, Nalivia will be able to protect herself and find charms that may benefit the residents of Arolsen. If Nalivia can find those charms, the people of Arolsen would no longer need Rowanda's charms or the evil king's rule. I am going along to make sure the evil king is no longer in power. I am sure he is a dark wizard, and he is the one who has opened a confluence and captured our citizens."

Beir spoke, "King Nashua is indeed evil. He has no compassion for his people. All that he does is for his own benefit and glory. He is cruel, even to his own people, and makes many of them work as hard as the slaves. I have seen him imprison and even put to death many of his own subjects for no apparent reason other than it pleased him to do so and show off his power. His own guards hate and fear him. They know he has black magic and will use it against them if they show any resentment. But Mother, he is a strong wizard, and without meaning disrespect, your powers are waning. How do you intend to confront him?"

"I don't want to alarm you, but I will not be confronting him alone. I will have Rowanda and Nalivia by my side. I know you think they are untrained, and it is too dangerous, but I will be instructing them on the journey, and I will put myself between them and King Nashua if necessary. You also will be along to protect them. I will expect you to follow my instructions without fail, no matter what you perceive, the consequences might be. Do you understand?" Emeraza asked.

"Mother, I have always obeyed you without question, and I will continue to do so. You are not only my mother, but you are the Head Elder, and I have sworn my allegiance to serving and protecting the Order. You know I will do as I am instructed," Beir said as he saluted his mother as his leader.

"I am not as certain as my husband, and I would think Scherra would also have questions as it is her granddaughter who will also be put into danger," Graciella said with Salitha moving to her side.

"Graciella, both Scherra and I know the dangers our granddaughters may face in Arolsen. If it were not for the fact that our world is being destroyed, we would not ask this of them. You know we love our granddaughters almost as much as you do. Nalivia is not at fault for the present situation, but King Nashua assaulted our country before this moment, as you well know. You and Nalivia's mother were not the only slaves taken. Remember all those years without Beirimor. It started way back then. We need to stop this now, and our only chance is with these two young women," Salitha reminded Graciella.

"Young women! They are not women. They are just girls!" screamed Graciella.

Salitha scolded, "You shame us, Graciella! Rowanda succeeded in saving your life. Now, you are undermining her abilities and Neslora's need for her. We have no choice, and you know that." Salitha's voice softened as she said the last words.

"I want to go, too, then," Graciella said through her tears. "I will not send my child into a dangerous situation without being there to protect her."

Sternly and without compassion, Emeraza said directly to Graciella, "You would be in the way. You are not going. Beir will be there to protect her as will I. End of the discussion!"

Graciella sat chastised and gathered herself. She wiped the tears from her face and glowered at her mother-in-law. Feeling defiant, she knew better than to say another word. Graciella knew she had no powers against the Elder sorceress. Never before had Graciella felt so helpless even including the time in King Nashua's prison.

Emeraza continued talking, taking her gaze from Graciella and turning her attention to the assembly at large. "I would like to leave for Arolsen by the crescent moon within two days. You need to have everything in order here on Neslora before the full moon. Rowanda and Nalivia's powers, as well as my own, will be strongest at the full moon. We will need to confront King Nashua then. That gives us two weeks to accomplish what all of us need to do. Nalivia will need to find charms and meet us at the palace city. Beir and Rowanda must find Boultori and get Rowanda's talismans back from him, and I must study and gather all the resources needed to overthrow the king. It leaves us barely enough time to accomplish all of what we need to do before returning. In the meantime, Salitha also has preparations that must be completed here while we are gone. She will explain her dream and what it means for Neslora."

Emeraza gave her attention to Salitha as she explained her dream and its meaning. She told how the remaining young apprentice sorceresses would be instrumental in protecting the two confluences that may be opened into Neslora from Arolsen. The men of their village would be stationed at each confluence along with two of the young girls to deal with an invasion of our land. Knowing the places, but not the time, meant the elder sorceresses would also divide and go with the apprentices to continue their education in the field. No one would be in luxury, as camps would need to be set up at each site.

The discussion and planning went on for hours. Graciella had excused herself from helping prepare Rowanda for the inevitable, being reminded by Emeraza not to put fear or negativity into the child's mind. Resentfully, but with new resolve, Graciella nodded to her elder and left the building. She knew in her heart that Emeraza was correct, and it was important for Rowanda to have the best mindset possible to deal with the approaching ordeal. It was important that Graciella give Rowanda confidence. It might be the only protection Graciella could give to her child.

Once home, Graciella told Rowanda everything that was said in the town hall between herself, her father, and the Elders. Graciella said gently to her daughter, "You have been to Arolsen before. What do you need to pack? You won't be able to carry much."

Rowanda knew from past experiences that a cloak with a hood was one of the most important things to take along with sandals. She thought about what else she might need and then said in a worried voice, "I only have two charms. I had four before. I don't know if I will only have half my powers with only two. Do you know?"

At just that moment, Salitha entered her room. She had come through the front door without knocking, as was her custom being Graciella's mother and Rowanda's grandmother. There were no closed doors between them ever.

"Rowanda, Emeraza needs you to return to the hall. It is exactly the matter you are expressing concern with your mother about right now that Emeraza wants to correct," Salitha said as she gently took Rowanda's hand to guide her back out to the town hall.

As they entered hand-in-hand, Emeraza was standing at the large table that held the left-over charms. "Rowanda, I need for you to come and see if any of these talismans will offer themselves to you. Come over and close your eyes and do as you did once before."

Rowanda walked to the table. She closed her eyes and allowed her arms to float in the air above the charms. She slowly moved them across the expanse of the table. Nothing seemed to happen.

"Rowanda, I want you to use just your right hand. Lower it until I say to stop," Emeraza instructed.

Rowanda put her left arm by her side and started to lower her right hand until she heard Emeraza say stop. "Now move your hand to the right slowly," Emeraza noted.

Doing as instructed, Rowanda now lets her right-hand float freely to the right side. "Ouch! Something bit me," Rowanda yipped.

"Good, pick it up," Emeraza commanded.

"It isn't one thing, Elder. It is two things I feel," Rowanda said with her eyes held shut.

Emeraza looked at the table, and she saw Rowanda was correct. One item had rolled beside another. It had not been there previously but seemed to move in place of its own accord.

"Pick them both up and hand them to me," Emeraza said curiously. She could hardly wait to see what the two items were that demanded to be chosen together.

"Open your eyes, Rowanda," Emeraza said as she stared down at the two charms lying side by side. "It appears that these two charms need to be used together. What we have here is a tiger's eye gem and a fang or a tooth of some sort. I can't tell if it is an animal or reptile tooth. It is larger than any snake's fang we have on Neslora, but it is smaller than most large mammals' teeth. I can't place where or what it might have come, but I guess that is not important. What is important is that the two charms want to be together. Odd...."

Placing the two charms into Rowanda's hand, she closed Rowanda's fingers around them. "What do you feel when you hold them together in your palm?" Emeraza asked out of curiosity.

"They are warm...and prickly. I feel tingling throughout my whole arm and down into my body. It even is tingly down to my toes," Rowanda said as she searched the strange new feeling throughout her entire being.

Handing Rowanda a velvet bag, Emeraza told her to place them inside the bag and keep it close to her heart. She suggested Salitha sew the velvet pouch inside Rowanda's undergarment so it would stay close to her at all times.

"But what will I do when I need to wash my undergarments?" Rowanda asked as any child might do.

"Don't be absurd, Child," Emeraza said. "Water won't hurt either of the charms, but you can always take them out of the pouch and put them into another one when you wash your clothes. Here, take another velvet pouch and sew it into your change of underclothing. Now, are you happy?" Emeraza said without humor.

Salitha took Rowanda by the shoulder, protecting her from further abuse and guided her out the door. "Come on, Rowanda, I will show you how to sew the pouches into your garments so they cannot be detected."

As they left, Emeraza chided herself. She just could not understand why she had so little patience. She had known that Rowanda was the child of her son since Rowanda was born. Her only defense was just that—she was trying to protect herself from the pain of losing her son, and Rowanda was a constant reminder of her own child's loss. But now, her son was returned alive and well, and it was Rowanda who had brought him home. Why could she not leave those old habits behind? Emeraza was determined to work on having a better relationship with her granddaughter. This trip to Arolsen might be a blessing in disguise.

CHAPTER FOUR

 The crescent moon would be low in the sky tonight. It was time for the party to leave. Everyone had a satchel packed. Rowanda and Nalivia had their charms protected on their person. Emeraza, too, had her talismans close to her heart. Worn and old, they still held some power but were only a dim reminder of the power they once possessed.

Emeraza took out her charms. They could all fit within her pouch. She never had a sword, dagger, or weapon amongst her arsenal. Her pouch held a diamond from the depths of the earth, a piece of coral from the sea, a maple tree seed pod or whirligig that floated to her on the day her charms chose her. The whirligig represented air though grounded in the earth. Her last charm that represented fire was more elusive. Only she, of all the young sorceresses, had a puff of smoke that stayed with her at all times. Her elders marveled that smoke could remain in her pouch and never dissipate. It was an enigma. None of the elders could explain how something like smoke could remain forever in that form. Emeraza's pouch always felt like a balloon, filled with air, but she knew it was not air, but her puff of smoke expanding in the pouch. On many occasions, she had willed the smoke into a blazing fire.

Rarely did Emeraza have the need for self-protection. Now, that could all change. Beirimor told her of the creatures inhabiting the desert, as well as the nomads who often meant others harm. The king, for sure, was a menace, and she would need all her powers to deal with him. How her talisman would come into play was not evident. Depending upon her own self-strength and years of wisdom, she hoped it would serve her well. Wise woman was what she was called.

Emeraza thought about what wisdom meant. She was known for applying soundness of action in regard to experience, knowledge, and judgment. People said Emeraza had fantastic common sense and was very shrewd. Knowing that people thought she had great powers of wisdom and keen mental discernment made her proud, but there was a nagging feeling that all her years of experience and her intelligence would be put to the test as never before on this trip. Would she fall short when she was most needed? She could not let self-doubt stop her from doing what must be done when the time came for her to act.

Putting all her fears aside, Emeraza packed and met the group to leave on their trek. Everyone was gathered and ready. They would use the confluence near the dried grass around the pond where Rowanda first went to Arolsen to find and return the abducted mothers. Once the group entered the confluence, Emeraza would close the portal forever.

Graciella wanted to accompany her husband and daughter to the opening, but Emeraza told her it would be too complicated for everyone. Tears and regrets were not helpful at the start of this journey. Graciella reluctantly stayed behind with her own mother and the mother and grandmother of Nalivia. They found comfort in each other's company as they watched the small group disappear into the trees.

Emeraza asked if everyone was ready to enter Arolsen. Nalivia hung back behind Beir. She and Emeraza had no idea of what they may encounter, but Nalivia, in particular, was fearful hearing tails of huge serpents and giant lizards. The fact that Arolsen had coalitions of large cats that hunted people made matters worse.

An opening became apparent, and Emeraza held the portal open while Rowanda entered first, followed by Nalivia. Beirimor stepped through and held out his arm to Emeraza to steady her as she stepped through the confluence. Rowanda was both amazed and pleased that her flower continued to mark the spot where she entered when she first arrived in Arolsen.

Beir smiled at the thought that this was the spot where he first met his daughter, even though he did not know Rowanda was his daughter at the time. Rowanda smiled at her father, remembering his scolding her for using the chalice of water and how the water would draw terpors or wetchels.

"I remember that we left quickly after you planted this flower. I wonder if there is a wetchel or terpor that stays in this area due to the flower even now?" Beir stated. "The creature would be drawn to the flower's moisture. Your magic is quite astounding that the flower to exist here in the desert after all this time."

"What do you mean that a terpor or wetchel could be in this area due to that flower?" asked Nalivia in apparent terror.

"We won't stay around to find out. Conceal your head and face and follow me," Beir directed.

Pulling their cloaks up over their head and covering all but their eyes, the group started out into the desert. Rowanda gave Nalivia and her grandmother hints as to how to stay in Beir's footsteps as they followed him up sand drifts. She knew both Nalivia and Emeraza would have trouble walking in the sand, especially as the day grew hotter.

Rowanda had just thought how cute it would be to have a drometarius to ride through the desert when she heard a familiar Grr Grr HREE sound. Beir stopped in his tracks and pulled out his sword. Rowanda stepped up beside him and quickly decided if her wand or sword would be her best choice. Not knowing why her hand left her belt and went to her chest where her two new charms were protected.

A large wetchel swung his head from side to side and whipped his tail towards Beir. Beir anticipated the strike and jumped aside. He stood between the giant lizard and Rowanda, brandishing his sword.

"Wait, Father," Rowanda yelled. "I want to see what my new charms will do to the wetchel. Let me try please."

Taking the two items into her hand, she focused their power on the giant lizard. Without hesitation, the lizard dropped to its belly and stayed motionless.

Rowanda cautiously walked towards the creature, who did not move a muscle. She slowly reached out and touched its tough, dry skin without it moving an inch.

"I think I killed it!" Rowanda said over her shoulder to Beir.

"No, you haven't killed him. Its eye is trained on you, and it is following your every movement. I think it is either stunned or it is submissive. I don't want to venture a guess as to which it may possibly be."

Emeraza stood completely immobile. She had heard the stories of wetchels, but until this moment, she had not really believed it could be true. There was nothing like this creature on Neslora, and Emeraza was glad that was the case.

"What do we do…run while it is frozen?" The elderly sorceress asked, lifting her cloak above her knees to make it easier to flee.

Rowanda, curious beyond caution, asked Beir to lift her up onto the gigantic lizard. She thought it would be much more helpful to get a ride through the desert than to walk.

"Uhmm, I am not sure that is a good idea, Rowanda. We don't really know how long this monster is going to stay calm. It could be he is playing possum and may strike at any moment. I think your grandmother's idea of running while he is motionless is a good idea," Beir said with what he thought was good judgment.

"No, really. I think this beautiful creature will let us ride on its back. I don't know why I think that, but it is almost like I can hear the creature inside my head." Rowanda started to jump to see if she could reach his back and the animal remained utterly motionless.

Beir watched and decided Rowanda may genuinely have a connection with this animal due to her talismans. He walked towards Rowanda and lifted her up on the wetchel's back. "Okay, what next?" Beir asked as he stepped back.

Rowanda thought about a forwarding motion, and the giant lizard rose to his feet and started to walk with Rowanda on its back.

"Wow! It is doing exactly as I am telling it to do mentally. It understands me! Come on. Get on its back," Rowanda shouted in glee.

"No way!" said Emeraza as she stepped back from the monster. Nalivia seconded her statement and hid behind the older woman.

Beir sized up the situation. "You have no idea how far we need to walk and how hot it is going to become. If Rowanda can control this creature, we will get where we need to go faster and safer. Few creatures in the desert will challenge a full-grown wetchel. I know you are afraid, but I am going to insist that you get on the lizard's back. I will help each of you. Rowanda, do you think you can have the wetchel lay down on its belly again. It would make it much easier for me to lift Nalivia and Emeraza up onto its back behind you," Beir asked.

Rowanda thought 'drop to your belly,' and the wetchel did as commanded. Beir then dragged Emeraza, his mother, to the wetchel's side and lifted her upon its back with her kicking and screaming. Nalivia was not much better, but Beir could handle her more effectively due to her diminutive size. With them up and secure, Beir leaped upon the creature and held the two squirming females in place.

"Mother, for an Elder sorceress, you certainly are fearful," Beir reprimanded his mother.

"I am only fearful of that which can harm those around me that I love," Emeraza responded.

"Yeah, right. You are probably afraid of mice and spiders, too," Beir teased.

"Okay, okay, stop squirming, or you will fall off. It is going to be a while until you feel comfortable with the wetchel's swaying movement the way it is. If you are wriggling around, it is going to make it so much harder for you to stay on when he starts running. Now settle down, both of you," Beir said with authority.

Both Emeraza and Nalivia obeyed Beir as he made it clear it was in their best interest to behave. "I think we are ready to go, Rowanda. I will tell you in what direction to head the wetchel since he will only hear and obey your thoughts."

Beir pointed in the general direction that they needed to go, and Rowanda let her gaze follow his hand signal. The wetchel immediately lumbered in the direction indicated by Rowanda's thoughts.

Riding the swaying lizard was difficult at first, but soon the four members of the group relaxed and allowed their bodies to get into synchronization with the wetchel's serpentine movements. There was no jostle as if riding most animals but a smooth undulation from side to side. After a short time, Nalivia honestly said it was fun. Even Emeraza relaxed.

What would have taken a day or more on foot, found the travelers approaching the oasis where Boultori and Beir had lived just a month prior. Wondering if Anarigar had remained this whole time, Beir's question was answered when the young man raced out from the flock of goats with a menacing spear in his hand.

Thinking 'stop' in her mind, Rowanda made the wetchel lay on his belly to Anarigar's surprise. Disbelief remained in his eyes, Anarigar did not lower his spear but stood his ground.

"Good evening, Anarigar," Beir said in the way of greeting. "Don't be too alarmed by our mode of travel. This wetchel will not hurt you as long as Rowanda is here. You can lower your spear. We have much to talk about with you."

Lifting Nalivia and Emeraza from the wetchel's back, Beir directed them to the first of many tents. "You will find cool water, dates, and pillows for you to rest upon. Please, go in and relax while I explain to Anarigar why we are here."

Emeraza and Nalivia gladly scampered to the tent with Nalivia giving Anarigar a glance as she passed him. She knew immediately this was the young man Rowanda had talked about from her first trip to Arolsen.

Rowanda slipped from the wetchel's back and asked of Beir, "Will we need the wetchel to travel tomorrow, or should I release him?"

Beir was undecided. It was so much easier to travel across the sand with the wetchel, and Emeraza was elderly. A long walk in the sand would be very hard on her.

"I think you should have the wetchel stay here. We can release our new found friend in the morning if we decide we would rather walk. Make sure he knows he can have water, but the goats are off-limits. They will be nervous just having the wetchel this close. In fact, it is better if we bring water to the wetchel and he stays in this spot."

Rowanda commanded the wetchel to lie down and stay. It did not seem that she needed to touch her charms to communicate with the beast any longer. Rowanda did wonder whether the influence would last over the night and whether the wetchel would be here in the morning. That was tomorrow's problem, but securing the goats was a problem for tonight just in case the wetchel came out of his trance.

Walking down to Anarigar, Beir commended him for staying to watch over their flock for a whole month. Anarigar explained that Boultori was probably in the palace city. Beir said he did not know if Boultori was a captive or if he was now the ruler and wondered if Anarigar had heard of a change in power.

Anarigar said he had talked with caravans coming through to water their drometarius at the well, but no one said that King Nashua was not on his throne. In fact, Anarigar told how travelers were surprised by the lush growth now circling the palace city. The palace-city was a vast oasis and people were now being forced to work in the fields and orchards. Many travelers said they left quickly for fear they would be enslaved to work as well.

Beir realized if King Nashua was in power, that meant Boultori was being held prisoner and ordered to create the gardens and fields that now surrounded the palace city. What was going to be a hard feat, had just become even more difficult.

CHAPTER FIVE

With the goats secured and the wetchel given water, the small band of people settled into the tent for an evening meal and to sleep. As they sat upon pillows, eating, Beir explained more to Anarigar.

At first, Anarigar was suspicious of the description of what a confluence was and how people came and went between two separate worlds. However, seeing Rowanda's ability to control a wetchel made Anarigar realize Rowanda was indeed a sorceress from another world. Since only men could be wizards in Arolsen, the explanation of another but the opposite world seemed logical.

Beir told Anarigar how Rowanda had given Boultori two of her charms, and that is what was being used to create the oasis around the palace city. Beir went on to tell Anarigar that each plant which sprouted in Arolsen killed a similar plant in Neslora and soon, Neslora would become a desert.

Beir asked Anarigar if he would be willing to accompany Nalivia on a mission to find charms from Arolsen that could be used to cause plants to grow in this world without affecting Neslora. With Nalivia sitting at Anarigar's feet, batting her eyelashes at him, the young man found it hard to say no.

Rowanda sat with Emeraza with contempt for Nalivia's obvious flirtation towards the young man who had caught Rowanda's attention on the first trip to Arolsen. 'How can Nalivia betray me like this. She knows I saw him first. I told her how cute I thought he was. She is supposed to be my best friend, and this is how she treats me. I cannot believe she has the nerve to try to steal him right before my eyes....' Rowanda's thoughts flowed.

Emeraza sensing her granddaughter's distress and anger, patted Rowanda's hand. Leaning close to Rowanda's ear, she whispered, "I can see why you are smitten with Anarigar. He is terrific looking and loyal. I see Nalivia thinks so, too. Remember, you are destined to be the next Elder Sorceress and men will only draw your attention away from what is important at this stage of your training."

Sitting back upon the pile of pillows, Emeraza snacked on another date. She smiled, remembering her own love triangle when she first met Beirimor's father. To this day, Alfinia bristles when Emeraza's husband's name is mentioned, even though he has been dead for fifteen years.

Rowanda allowed herself to ponder what her grandmother said. It was hard to imagine that she may be the Elder in the community at some point. Rowanda wondered why her grandmother seemed so sure she would be the one to fill her shoes. There were six other apprentices at present, and soon more girls could possibly show signs of being sorceresses. Rowanda made a mental note to ask her grandmother at a later date why Emeraza felt she would be the chosen one, but not now with Beir talking to Anarigar.

Anarigar spoke. "We will need to drive the flock of goats to my father's tents. They cannot stay unattended for any amount of time. Will you accompany me, or will you go directly to the palace city and Nalivia and I will meet you there?"

"I believe a wetchel driving the flock would only create chaos. It is better if you and Nalivia drive the herd. We will stay an extra day to allow Emeraza to rest," Beir said.

"I don't need an extra day to rest. I rode all the way here. It is not as if I walked in the hot sand most of the day. I think we can proceed to the palace city tomorrow. It is better that we find where Boultori is being held prisoner. The sooner we are able to retrieve the chalice and pouch of seeds, the less destruction will occur in Neslora. That is my number one concern!" Emeraza said with emphasis.

"I guess it is settled. You and Nalivia will take the herd to your father's tents. From there, Nalivia will need to use her instincts to search and find the charms to assist Boultori to make Arolsen lush and green," Beir said.

With trepidation, Nalivia asked Emeraza, "How am I to know when I find a charm, Elder?"

Emeraza motioned Nalivia to come to her. "Nalivia, child, your charms are special. I knew the moment your own teardrop chose you, that it had a special purpose. I believe if you use your teardrop with the prism talisman, you will know without a doubt when you find a charm. I think you will only need to find several. I am certain earth, air, water, and fire will be the basis for charms on Arolsen as they are for us on Neslora. It seems Neslora and Arolsen are one and the same but opposites."

"I don't understand how two things can be the same and opposite at the same time. If I am to find charms that will provide lush vegetation here on Arolsen, why won't their use cause deserts in the corresponding area of Neslora?" Nalivia questioned.

"I'm sorry to confuse you. The opposite is not the word I wanted, but mirror images are probably closer to what I am trying to say. It is all very abstract and mystical, so it is more my intuition than fact. Does that help you understand?"

"Not really, Elder, but I will think upon what you said. Maybe after a good night's sleep, everything will seem clearer," Nalivia said without much conviction.

Rowanda listened to what her grandmother told Nalivia. Having been here before, Rowanda was aware that Arolsen and Neslora were completely opposite but, at the same time, similar. She could not explain to Nalivia either what she knew, but it did not make it less real.

In the morning, Rowanda was no happier than she was the previous night when she saw Nalivia dancing around Anarigar as they packed to leave. Feeling petty, Rowanda kept her distance from Nalivia as her friend prepared to go. It seemed Nalivia was utterly unaware of how Rowanda felt as Nalivia left without even saying goodbye.

"Harumph!" Rowanda said under her breath.

"You know Boultori would be laughing hard at your distress if he was here. I can just about hear him saying, 'Little Dragon, are you going to lay down and be walked upon like a carpet. If you want Anarigar, why don't you fight for him?'" Beir said, mimicking Boultori's voice as he prepared to leave the tent.

"Beirimor, don't encourage Rowanda's childish fantasy. You know as well as I do that she is fated to be the next Elder. She needs to keep her wits about her, and that boy will just be a distraction," Emeraza chided her son.

"Yes, Mother," Beir said as he gave Rowanda a wink before lifting the flap of the large Bedouin tent and exiting.

"Foolishness!" Emeraza exclaimed to Rowanda.

The two continued to sort through their satchels to make sure everything was in place. Previously, before leaving the tent, Beir asked his mother to prepare food for the journey. Rowanda was to fill their water flasks.

Rowanda went outside to fill the flasks from the well and watched as Anarigar drove the goats out into the open desert with Nalivia skipping along beside him as if she was a playful puppy.

'Surely, Anarigar will find Nalivia to be a foolish, little girl and tire of her antics after a day or two,' thought Rowanda as she allowed her eyes to linger on the couple heading away from her. 'I see now that I have grown up, and Nalivia is still a child.' Rowanda continued her mental conversation with herself trying hard to bolster her own ego now that it was feeling bruised as Anarigar seemed infatuated with her *ex*-best friend.

"Your wetchel could use some water as well before we leave," said Beir, waking Rowanda from her ruminating thoughts.

Rowanda startled, not hearing Beir's approach. Beir noticed where Rowanda's gaze was directed. He wanted to give advice to his daughter, but being away for so many years and not even knowing he had a daughter, left him without experience. Instead, he gave her a sizeable oiled bag to offer water to the giant lizard and said nothing.

Rowanda had all but forgotten the wetchel with her thoughts fixated on Nalivia and Anarigar. "Oh, right, the wetchel..." Rowanda said, "I almost forgot about it. It is amazing the lizard remained where I left it. The wetchel hasn't moved a muscle, has it? Maybe the night's air was too cold for the reptile. I should have thought to make sure it had some warmth—a blanket or something. How thoughtless I have been towards the creature."

"Yes, reptiles don't do well in the cold, but it seems to be alive and fit to travel. We will only need it for one more day, and then you can release it," Beir said as he studied the animal. "Go see if your grandmother is ready to travel."

Giving Beir the flasks she just filled, Rowanda scurried back down to the tent. Emeraza was just coming out of the tent when Rowanda arrived.

"Are you ready to travel, Elder?" Rowanda asked with respect.

"You may call me Grandmother, Rowanda," Emeraza said quickly in reply. "When we are back in the community, and we are in assembly, you need to call me Elder, but at any other time, I would prefer you to call me Grandmother."

Startled, but pleased, Rowanda said, "Yes, Grandmother." Taking the basket from her grandmother's hand, Rowanda followed Emeraza to the waiting wetchel.

Emeraza stiffened momentarily as she approached the wetchel. She had already forgotten how large and fierce the animal appeared up close. Reinforcing her confidence, she walked right up to the animal and prepared herself for Beir's assistance to mount.

Rowanda went to the giant lizard's face and stroked it. "Thank you, Faris, for another day's service."

"Faris? You are naming the wetchel, now?" Beir asked his daughter with a smile forming on his lips. He was sure this was just his daughter acting like a little girl, naming a pet.

"That is his name, Father. I didn't make it up. He told me his name. It means knight, like a protector," Rowanda said matter-of-factly.

Beir rubbed his head in puzzlement and looked up at his mother to catch her reaction. A smug smile cross Emeraza's face. "I told you she would take my place as the next Elder. Did you doubt me? She is special. But then again, with a sorceress on both sides of the family, how could she not...but be special?"

Lifting Rowanda up in front of her grandmother, Beir jumped on the back. Once again, he positioned himself to assist his mother if the going got rough.

"We are ready to go if Faris is ready," Beir said to his daughter. "You will need to head him to the north. We must release him before we are in sight of the palace city."

The wetchel sprung to his feet and set out at a quick pace. Emeraza found herself being flung back into her son's chest as the wetchel's speed caught her unprepared. Soon, she was swaying with the undulation of the animal's side-to-side movements.

The day became hot quickly. It was difficult to keep one's hood up over the head with the speed the wetchel traveled. Beir kept his eyes moving across the desert, fearful a terpor could rise up out of the sand at any moment. Terpor often attacked wetchels for the same reason wetchels attacked most anything else living. The lizard's body was full of water, and the desert serpent's keen nostrils could detect even small amounts of moisture.

Seeing the sand rise in a long column, Beir knew he was wise to watch for a terpor. The serpent was not that far away, but Beir could not immediately decide if the serpent was heading towards them or not.

"Rowanda, I don't want to alarm you, but I see evidence of a terpor to the left. I am not sure if he is coming towards us or not. If he is, it would be best if you ask Faris to speed up and outrun the snake. I don't want to have a battle. I am not sure which one of the two creatures would win, but I suspect the terpor would win since it is poisonous," Beir shouted over the wind.

Rowanda turned her head to the left and noticed the sand's movement and knew the terpor was indeed tracking them. She mentally communicated to the wetchel to run faster.

The wetchel surprised all of the humans by springing to his hind legs and running on his back two feet at an incredible speed. Rowanda was unaware that the lizard could do such a feat and held on with all her might. Beir, too, adjusted his position quickly and grabbed Emeraza as she shifted to one side and nearly slid off the back of the wetchel.

Keeping an eye on the mound of sand, Beir was relieved to see it was no longer gaining on the fleeing wetchel. Allowing the creature to run at full speed for as long as it was able, everyone, including the lizard seemed exhausted when Faris finally returned to all fours and lessened his pace to a more comfortable trot.

"What in the world was chasing us that the wetchel needed to run that fast?" gasped Emeraza.

"That, my dear mother, was a terpor. I am glad the wetchel surprised us with that burst of speed. You would not have liked meeting a terpor!" Beir barked into his mother's ear.

Beir could feel his mother shiver even though the temperature was over 100 degrees. He knew the shiver did not mean she was cold but scared witless. Having faced a terpor more than once, living in the desert for all those many years, Beir always dreaded the next encounter. How he had managed to escape death on the several occasions of encountering them, was not only luck but tutelage from his dear friend Boultori. He owed the man much.

Stopping abruptly, Beir shouted to his daughter for an explanation. Rowanda pointed to the cloud of dust.

"Darn! I was hoping we would not encounter any nomads on this trip," Beir shouted.

"Father, Faris is too exhausted to outrun them. I am suggesting that we release him to go find a spot where he can recuperate. I have no intention of running him to death. He has been a good friend, and I can't allow him to die for us. Maybe if he leaves, the krerri will track him and not us," Rowanda said as she slipped off the wetchel.

Beir was not sure Rowanda was making a good choice, but he could not feel the animal's distress, so he trusted his daughter. Offering assistance to Emeraza, Beir stabilized the elderly woman as she found her feet.

Rowanda went to the wetchel's head and patted him. She leaned her head, touching his head, and communicated her thoughts. The wetchel moved off with a backward glance, stopped and hesitated before moving on again, which Beir interpreted as the wetchel's reluctance to leave Rowanda.

"I suggest that we move to the far side of the sand drift and cover ourselves completely. I will cover you and my mother with sand and hope that will help to camouflage our presence," Beir suggested.

The three of them ran to the other side of the sand drift. Covering the women's faces with their cloak, Beir used his hands to cover the rest of them with sand, hiding them completely. Beir then covered himself as best as he could and whispered for Rowanda and Emeraza to be as quiet as possible.

Emeraza knew she must be quiet, but her old bones were aching from being curled up in a fetal position. She wanted nothing more than to stretch and move the sand from her face. The feeling of suffocation was becoming unbearable even though she knew she was not going to die from lack of oxygen.

Panic was starting to set in when she heard a crunching and snuffling sound indicating the animals tracking them were close. With renewed vigilance to be silent and motionless, Emeraza lay as quiet as possible, fearing to move even an inch. She held her breath, hoping to seem invisible.

A growl close to Emeraza's ear left no doubt that the large cats had found her hiding place. "Don't move, Grandmother," Emeraza heard Rowanda say in a calm, quiet voice.

Sitting up, Rowanda faced five krerri. Their golden eyes were locked on her own. Rowanda could see the sand shift where Beir had buried himself. "Don't move, Father, until I tell you to do so," Rowanda whispered.

Rowanda slowly allowed her right hand to touch the pouch sewn into her undergarment. Just the lightest touch was enough for the five krerri to react. Their eyes softened, and their hackles lowered until all the fur was smooth again. Purring began, and the five large cats came to Rowanda's side. As she stood, the animals began to rub themselves on her body as if they were house cats.

"I think it is safe for you to stand now," Rowanda said to her father and Grandmother, as she found herself stroking the animal's coats. Immediately, the animals started to chirp. It was clear the cats were feeling some confusion as to whether the other two humans were threats to the girl.

Sending calming thoughts as Rowanda had done with the wetchel provided the same results. Rowanda could feel the cats in her mind. She knew what they were feeling, and she knew how to impress her thoughts upon them.

"It is okay. These krerri won't hurt you," Rowanda said with confidence.

"Are you sure?" Emeraza asked as she stepped behind her son.

"Yes, I am totally sure. They are not afraid of us. We are no threat to krerri, and the beasts know it. I just am not sure how the nomads are going to respond. I don't have a talisman to communicate with them. Unfortunately, they see us as a way to make a profit. I am not so sure we can convince them not to sell us as slaves," Rowanda said with fear creeping into her voice.

The big cats sensed Rowanda's fears and formed a circle around her, growling and preparing for battle. Not knowing who the enemy might be, the cats seemed nervous and excitable.

Beir quietly suggested, "Rowanda, calm yourself. You are making the krerri nervous, and I am not sure that they don't perceive your grandmother and myself as the threat you are feeling. They don't seem to understand you are afraid of the nomads. I don't think they can think of abstracts."

Rowanda took a deep breath. "What do you suggest we do when the nomads find us?"

"I don't think we have long before we find out. I hear the nomads drometarius now!" Beir said with his voice less composed than he had hoped it would be.

Shrieks, yells, and yodels filled the air as the nomads advanced to see what the krerri had surrounded. Running down the sand drift with weapons held ready, they were staggered to find the five krerri between them and their victims. The krerri growled and spit, lunging with jaws snapping and claws extended to do damage.

Halting, the handlers advanced slowly, commanding the krerri to obey and come to their sides with no results. The krerri remained between the controllers and the girl, menacing the handlers as they held their hands out to grab the collars each animal wore.

"He bit me!" screamed one handler. "My krerri bit me. I raised him from a cub. He has never bit me before! What is the meaning of this? The girl must be an enchantress. Shoot her, shoot her with an arrow!"

With bows and menacing arrows drawn and leveled at Rowanda's heart, a booming voice was heard, "Stop! Do not harm her!"

CHAPTER SIX

 A tall man, wearing an expensive and colorful sleeveless cloak worn over a tunic, with a distinct headcloth, came forward. "Do not hurt the child. They will be our guests. Set up camp and prepare a feast. I wish to converse with the travelers alone in my tent."

Without hesitation, the whole band moved in a flurry of activity, setting up tents, staking out the drometarius, and preparing a feast. The commander of the nomads indicated that the three people should accompany him to his tent. The krerri flanked Rowanda and would not be persuaded to leave her side as their handlers tried to coax and entice them with food.

"Leave the krerri. Let the beasts stay with the girl," the leader commanded.

"So, Child, you must be an enchantress. Tell me about yourself," said the Chieftain as he indicated a spot for the three to sit. Clapping his hands, several women wearing sheer blue fustans with red embroidery came in carrying food and drink. Serving each guest, the wine was poured, dates and goat cheese was placed on small serving tables. As the ladies left, jingling sounds were heard as their silver bracelets, and anklets brightened the tent with musical notes.

"Rowanda is not old enough to drink wine, Sir," Beir said as respectfully as possible. "Might there be juice from the grape or even goats milk for her instead?"

"We have watered it down. It will not affect Rowanda, but if you would prefer, I will order something else for her to drink." Again, the Chieftain clapped his hands, and a pitcher of cool scented water was placed by Rowanda's side.

Sipping from the chalice, Rowanda found the liquid to be refreshing and wondered what the unfamiliar taste may be. She was sure it was some exotic fruit juice mixed with the water, like mango or some berries. Whatever it was, she found it delicious.

"You are enjoying the liquid refreshment. I am glad it pleases you," boomed the voice of their host.

"Please, relax. My name is Prince al-Djitu. I am the emir of my people. And how should I address you?" the prince said with a joyful look on his face.

Beir felt he should be the one to introduce the two females, not knowing how the nomads looked upon women. Beir had limited encounters with the women of Arolsen since he was held in the slave quarters with other men, and once he escaped, he stayed as far away as possible. Most of the women traveling with caravans seemed protected and out of sight most of the time, except to draw water from his well.

"Prince al-Djitu, I would like to introduce my mother, the Elder Emeraza and her apprentice, my daughter, Rowanda," Beir said with pride.

"The title Elder I am familiar with as we also have elders in our tribe which we revere. However, I think I must be mistaking what the title means to you since our elders never have apprentices. They may have slaves, but not anyone who will learn skills from them. If I understand, your mother must possess skills that need to be passed down to your daughter. Am I correct? If so, what are these skills?" Prince al-Djitu asked politely but without hiding his curiosity.

Beir looked to his mother to see if she felt he should hide her talent or if she thought the prince would be impressed, knowing she was a powerful sorceress. The look exchanged did not go unnoticed by the prince.

Turning to Emeraza, he asked pointedly. "Should I address you as your highness?"

"Elder is fine. In my land, I am considered a sorceress. Since I am the head sorceress, I am given the respected title of Elder. Rowanda is just learning her skills. Someday, she will take my place as Elder, but for now, she is my apprentice and granddaughter. As you have seen, she already possesses great powers." Emeraza indicated the five krerri curled up by Rowanda's feet or sitting protectively beside her.

"Yes!" with a deep belly laugh, "I was very impressed with her abilities to charm the hunters of our tribe. We have raised them since cubs and never has one ever shown defiance before to their handlers. In fact, no one but their handlers has ever touched them, and there they sit like house cats from the palace. Remarkable. Would you share your magic with us?" the prince said with his smile not reaching his eyes.

Beir felt something sinister in the last question asked. He wanted to deflect the subject quickly.

"At present, Prince al-Djitu, we have another apprentice who is searching for charms that can be used by wizards from your world. Our own charms cannot be used in this world except by the women that the charms have chosen. Do you possess the ability to practice wizardry? If so, when we meet with our apprentice, she will have charms available for your use." Beir said.

"I have a wizard. I am not one myself, but I do not need to be one when I have one available to me. I will call my wizard." The prince clapped his hands, and a guard came quickly to his side. With two words spoken, the guard left. Momentarily, he returned, opening the flaps of the tent to admit a tall man with a black mustache and beard with streaks of gray.

"You sent for me, my prince?" the man said with a sweeping bow.

The prince introduced his wizard, "Arefer, I would like to present the Elder Emeraza and her apprentice, Rowanda, along with their guard. Elder Emeraza is a powerful sorceress. Even her apprentice shows great powers as her ability to charm our krerri testifies. Do you think your skills are greater?"

Looking down at the two seated females, Arefer dismissed them, saying, "These are mere women. They are no match for me. I could outmaneuver the Elder with one hand tied behind my back and without my wand."

"Then, we shall have a show tonight. I think my people would like a demonstration of your powers versus my wizard's magical talents. It is settled."

Clapping his hands, the prince summoned many guards and told them to set up an arena where all the people could watch. Build fires so everyone can see. Quickly, I want the show to start without delay."

The guards raced out of the tent, and a flurry of activity was heard as people ran from place to place, grabbing one item or another. A giant bonfire could be seen with sparks rising into the dark and starlit sky.

"What is that awful smell," Emeraza asked while plugging her nose.

"That dear Mother," Beir said with a wicked smile, "is drometarius droppings. The nomads use it as fuel to make fires here in the desert."

Emeraza looked towards Beir. "I am not sure what you have gotten us into this time. I don't do magic to entertain. This is beneath my dignity!"

Beir walked closer to Emeraza. "I don't think this display is for entertainment. I have a feeling that this competition could decide our fates. If we win, we may be able to walk away, but if Arefer proves to be more powerful, we will probably become slaves.... What do you have up your sleeve, Mother?"

As the Prince indicated it was time to go out to the arena, several handlers came into the tent with ropes and muzzles to secure the krerri. Hissing, snarling and warning the controllers to stay back with swipes of their paws, did little to keep the men away. Soon, the krerri were leashed and muzzled and led away much to Rowanda's dismay. "Don't hurt them!" Rowanda cried after the handlers.

Walking out into the night, Rowanda saw easily two hundred men, women, and children seated around an expanse of open space with a platform in the middle. The guards gently pushed the three guests towards the platform. Arefer was waiting on the stage.

Prince al-Djitu announced that the festivities were about to begin. He stepped aside, clapping his hands in joy while guards assisted him down the stairs of the make-shift stage.

Arefer brought out his wand and a stream of fire shot from the end of it. He stepped back, waiting for Emeraza to meet his challenge. Instead, Emeraza pushed Rowanda to the center and told her to use her wand to create fire, too. Rowanda, unpracticed, held her wand out in front of her and fire leaped forward, traveling a further distance from her wand, catching several tents on fire.

"Oh my gosh! I am so sorry!" yelled Rowanda as many men ran to get water to put out the fires.

Arefer angrily said that the child was a menace. The prince just howled in laughter. "She did match your magic, Arefer, and she is only an apprentice. Can't you show us something better than fire from your wand?" Prince al-Djitu heckled.

Ruffling with indignation, Arefer once again used his wand and caused a wall of spears to surround the trio, imprisoning them within the shafts. Without thinking of the ramifications, Rowanda grabbed her sword, closed her eyes, and thought 'whirling wind.' A cyclone budded from her sword, lifting each spear from the canvas floor, rapidly, one at a time, sending each as a hurling weapon above the seated crowds and landing forcefully into erected tents in all directions, including the prince's own tent. Thunk! Thunk! Thunk! Thunk was heard as each spear hit its target.

Turning bright red with anger, Arefer raised his wand to immobilize the three with his freezing magic, but not before Rowanda put her hand to her heart, clutching her pouch with her two new charms. Not being able to move a muscle, Rowanda used her mind and reached out to all creatures living far and near.

Arefer, feeling vindicated with his skillful containment of the three other bodies on the stage, turned to bow to the crowd with gales of laughter, whoops, and other noises of delights. Turning to Prince al-Djitu, he exclaimed, "I am more powerful than these pathetic sorceresses. You may do with them as you wish. I suggest you sell them as slaves and get them out of my sight."

Prince al Djitu was about to make a statement or maybe a command when the sand started to vibrate as if there was an earthquake. The people jumped from their seated positions and began to scream in fear. Many were about to flee to their tents when they realized the whole encampment was surrounded by giant terpor. As many as one hundred serpents encircled the nomads, hissing, and striking if any got close. All the people backed further and further away from the serpents until they were crowded tightly next to the stage.

Fear gripped the prince, and he yelled for Arefer to release the sorceresses immediately. "I said now! Arefer, you fool! What have you done? You will get us all killed!"

Arefer grappled for his wand. Dropping it twice in his haste to do as the prince commanded, stuttering, he said his magic words to release the immobilization spell.

Rowanda, Emeraza, and Beir were once again able to move. Emeraza's eye widened at the sight of the hundred gigantic serpents swaying, hissing and striking to keep the whole nomad camp confined in one place.

"Do something, Sorceress!" Prince al-Djitu pleaded.

Beir shoved Rowanda forward. "You summoned these creatures. Only you can dismiss them. Go on and do your magic."

Rowanda stepped down from the platform. The crowd parted as best as they could to allow her to pass even though they were packed so tightly together that movement was painful.

Rowanda came face to face with the first serpent, who rose up into the air seven feet high. Rowanda patted the snake's skin and whispered, "Go in peace." and the serpent dropped his head and slithered away. It took many minutes for Rowanda to go to each and every serpent, saying the same words with the same results. When the serpents had dug back under the sand and vanished in every direction, the nomads quietly slipped back into their tents, some pulling out the spears before entering.

The prince humbly asked the trio to return to his tent. Arefer was dismissed with a flick of the hand.

"Your magic must be great if your apprentice is so powerful. I bow before you and ask your mercy on my people." Prince al-Djitu said as he dropped to his knees in their presence.

Emeraza took the prince by his hand and asked him to rise. "We mean you no harm. We truly are here to help your people. King

Nashua has something that belongs to my apprentice. We are here to get it back, but King Nashua is an evil man. It may take more than the three of us to defeat the king if we are not to hurt any innocent people. We feel the king has hurt his own people long enough, and we do not want to do more harm. Would you help us and go against the king?"

CHAPTER SEVEN

 Boultori labored every day at his brother's whim. The king made the guards take Boultori out each day to use his magic chalice and pouch of seeds to grow lush gardens for the king's entertainment. Not happy with having his courtyards filled with flowers and fruit trees, the king demanded more. He wanted fields and orchards to bring in more coffers into his pockets. When Boultori said the fields should be for the people's good, the king only laughed.

"The people can have as much food as they can pay for and nothing more. This is not a charity. If people are hungry and they can't pay for food, then they will work in my fields and orchards, and I will give them enough food for the day." King Nashua answered.

"You make me *slave* every day, and no one benefits except for you. That is wrong. You have always been selfish and a tyrant. If I were king, my people would eat as well as I do…" Boultori said to his brother.

"But you aren't king, now are you? What a soft, stupid king you would be. A king needs to be strong and rule with an iron fist. You, little brother, are a fool, and you will never be anything more than a fool. Take him back to his cell and put him in chains," barked the king to his guards.

As the guards led Boultori away, Boultori could not resist getting in the last word to his brother, "Mother always liked me best!"

The king was livid. "Make sure my brother gets no food tonight or tomorrow morning. Get him up at the first light of dawn and make sure Boultori plants no less than five-hectares."

Boultori was chuckling as he was led back to his cell. He knew he would pay for his last remark, but he didn't care. His brother was a bully and a jerk, and he always had been. As the chains were tightened around his wrists and ankles, Boultori slumped down on the bed of straw that was provided for him to sleep upon. He had slept on worse.

He remembered many nights curled up in the sand. He wondered what Beir was doing right now. He missed his friend. For years they hid out in the desert with only each other and the goats for company. It was a joy to have Rowanda amongst them. He remembered how much he loved to tease and torment the little girl. Calling her Little Dragon was much fun. However, Rowanda pretended offense even though she knew Boultori was not bullying her.

As Boultori settled himself to sleep as best as he could with both arms and legs chained to the walls, he thought about the moment Rowanda thrust the chalice and pouch of seeds into his hands before the confluence closed around her. That courageous little girl's last thoughts were about him and doing something good for his people. He admitted to himself that he missed the Little Dragon, and Boultori missed Beirimor even more.

The month since they had disappeared, back to their own world, was very difficult for Boultori. The guards immediately took him into custody once the Neslorian women were rescued. His brother, King Nashua, held Boultori responsible and was about to have him executed when one guard stepped forward with the chalice and pouch of seeds.

"What is that?" the king demanded of the guard.

The guard answered without hesitation, "Your Highness, I witnessed these two items being passed to Boultori as the prisoners escaped through the hole. I believe they are valuable."

King Nashua signaled the guard to bring the chalice and seeds to his throne, where he was seated. He turned the chalice in every direction imaginable, including upside down. Opening the pouch, the king poured out seeds into his palm.

"So, brother, tell me about these items, or I will have you beheaded where you stand." King Nashua glared at Boultori.

The guards brought Boultori closer to the throne and shoved him down on his knees. Poking Boultori with his spear, the guard reiterated what the king had said, "The king is waiting. Tell him what you know!"

Boultori rubbed his ribs where the spear had made an impression without tearing his clothing. "Be careful of my fine raiment. You might tear the cloth. Besides, if you puncture my lungs, I might explode, and you wouldn't want the king to have my guts all over him."

"Don't play the fool, Boultori. I have heard your ridiculous prattle all my life. It might have amused our mother, but it bores me to death." King Nashua said unkindly.

Boultori retorted, "I now have the secret to assassinate you. All I need to do is continue my nonsense, and you will die from boredom."

A guard came over without a signal from the king and kicked Boultori in the rump, knocking him face down on the floor in front of the king.

"Prostrating yourself before me will not save you from being executed. The only thing that might save your life is for you to tell me why you were given these two items." King Nashua inspected his fingernails and watched Boultori under veiled eyes.

"I grow tired. Guards, bring the executioner and tell him not to bother with sharpening his ax." King Nashua said with a vicious snarl on his lips. "You know a dull ax can take many tries before it severs your head from your body. It seems to be quite painful."

Boultori knew his brother would not spare him just because they shared the same mother and father. Boultori recognized his brother to be without compassion. As the executioner pushed the doors open to enter the throne room, Boultori found his tongue.

"If you must know, Brother, these two items are magic. They were given to me by a sorceress from Neslora so that I might grow plants to help our people have a better life. With them, I can produce fruit trees, flowering plants, and crops." Boultori finally said.

"I am a wizard. I should be able to use these magic charms without you. I may as well have your head to use as fertilizer for the plants I will grow." King Nashua said without moving his eyes from the chalice he held.

"I am afraid you will not be able to use them at all. The charms come from Neslora, and they will not work in Arolsen except by me. They were gifted to me, and only I can use them." Boultori said, not really knowing if he was speaking the truth or not.

King Nashua got to his feet and went to the window. He took one seed from the pouch and dropped it to the ground below. Tipping the chalice to provide water, King Nashua was frustrated when no water appeared. When nothing happened, he threw the chalice on the palace floor and stomped on it. Seeing not even a single dent, the king kicked the chalice to the tapestry-covered wall.

"Bring my brother to the window," commanded King Nashua. "Show me that you can produce a plant, and I will let you live."

Boultori took the pouch and chalice from the King. Boultori held his breath, hoping he was correct in his assessment that the chalice and seeds would work for him since Rowanda had bequeathed them to Boultori's keeping. Dropping one seed, he watched as it drifted to the ground below the window. Pouring water from the chalice directly onto the seed, Boultori waited, but only for a few seconds before a sprout pushed itself up from the soil and started to grow. Faster than what was imaginable, a robust and flexible plant grew up towards the sunlight, with leaves shooting out from the stem. Soon a bud appeared, and a lovely red rose blossomed. King Nashua was surprised when water emerged from the chalice.

King Nashua looked down at the results and remarked, "My, but that is a lovely rose bush. Take my brother outside and spend the rest of the afternoon in the courtyard. By the end of the day, I want to see roses blooming in every space available, aside from the area where my lovely wife may want to sit. In fact, ask my wife to supervise the planting of her garden. Tomorrow, I will have another project to keep my brother busy."

As Boultori was led from the throne room, he could not miss the dark, angry look in his brother's eyes. Boultori knew someone would pay the price for King Nashua's inability to use the chalice and seeds. As the door began to close behind him, Boultori heard the thunderous voice of his brother demanding the head of the guard who had brought the chalice and pouch of seeds to his attention. Sadly, Boultori knew his fate and the guards.

So, went Boultori's days for weeks. Every morning, the guards took him outside with legs shackled to work on whatever project the king demanded. The courtyards were all in bloom, an orchard was planted for the king's use only. Crops were now surrounding the palace walls, and townsmen were forced to work from sunrise to sunset with just a meager amount of food given in payment. The townsmen complained that their own jobs were suffering and their families were doing without because of the king's demands on their time.

Boultori heard his guards talking about the king planning another raid on Neslora to bring slaves to work his fields to allow his townsmen to return to their own jobs. Boultori went about listening to what the guards said, hoping there could be a means for his escape as well. Being able to escape to Neslora and take the chalice and pouch of seeds back to Rowanda seemed to be in his best interest. Being his brother's slave for the rest of his life did not seem to be what Boultori had in mind.

CHAPTER EIGHT

Anarigar had no idea in which direction to take Nalivia in her quest for charms for his world. The desert was the desert. It was all much the same no matter which direction one went. Suddenly, Anarigar remembered his grandfather talking about a sacred mountain two-days walk from their encampment. Anarigar decided if there were charms to be found, probably the mountain would contain them.

Anarigar's father allowed his son to take two drometarius for the journey. The animals' humps were filled. Both of the outer two humps held water while the middle hump contained the gelatinous substance the drometarius converted to food for the long journey.

Anarigar asked Nalivia if she could ride. "I rode on a wetchel, didn't I? I doubt the drometarius will be any more difficult," Nalivia said sweetly.

Anarigar grew tired of the girl's feeble attempts at flirtation. He was growing weary of her silliness and wished he did not need to escort her on her quest for talismans, but if it benefited his world, he would do as he was asked. He was honor-bound to fulfill his duty. Anarigar knew his father felt he owned Boultori and Beir much for the continued use of their well. As a son, that duty extended to himself.

Having the drometarius kneel so the girl could mount, Anarigar assisted the process with some annoyance at Nalivia's giggles and batting eyelashes. A part of Anarigar wished Rowanda would have been the one to seek the charms instead of her best friend. He wondered why Nalivia was the one chosen but decided it was not his business to know.

"Are you secure and ready for the drometarius to get to his feet?" Anarigar asked the girl.

"I am ready." Nalivia said, followed by, "Yikes! I didn't realize I would be rocked back and forth so badly when he got to his feet. You should have warned me that I would be thrust forward and backward so much. I almost came off this creature."

Anarigar rolled his eyes. Nalivia was tucked between the first and middle hump. There was no way she could have fallen off as the animal got to his feet. Her exaggeration and complaining only served to make Anarigar want to travel many steps ahead of the girl so as not to be able to listen to her incessant chatter.

Taking the lead, Anarigar headed the drometarius in the direction of the mountains, which could be seen faintly in the far distance. The mountains almost appeared to be a mist instead of solid. He knew as they grew closer and closer, the mountain would take on the shape of a horned lizard with several peaks forming that shape. Anarigar asked his father if he would be punished by walking on the sacred mountain.

Anarigar remembered his father's reply, "No, my son, as long as your intentions are good. The mountain spirits will know, and they will judge...."

'Judge what?' Anarigar wanted to ask but was afraid to hear his father's response, so he left the question unanswered. Anarigar thought his intentions were good. How could helping Beir and Rowanda be anything but good? They both said the charms would benefit his people. All Anarigar wanted was for his family to have a better life and not to struggle in the desert. Wishing that for all the people of his world could not be construed as anything but good, he hoped.

Knowing the trip would take two days, Anarigar let himself settle back upon his drometarius' hump to doze. The animal would continue to travel the straight line he was being directed towards unless something unusual would happen. Anarigar knew the animal would give a warning if a wetchel, terpor, nomad, or sandstorm should interrupt the day. Unfortunately, he had not factored in Nalivia.

"Help! Help!" was the cry that woke Anarigar.

Looking back towards the girl's distress call, Anarigar saw her drometarius in a full gallop heading at a diagonal to his own mounts path. Something had spooked the drometarius, but Anarigar saw nothing out of the ordinary.

Using his whip on his drometarius' hindquarters, Anarigar drove his animal into a full gallop as well. He chased after the girl and finally coming alongside her mount, he leaned to the side and grabbed the reins and pull the drometarius to a stop.

"What happened?" shouted Anarigar to the frightened girl.

"I don't know. I just started to sing when this crazy animal made an awful sound and started running. I can't imagine what scared him so badly. Is there a terpor around that you can see?"

Anarigar was quite sure there was no terpor or his own drometarius would have signaled an alarm as well. The only thing that could have frightened the drometarius was Nalivia's singing voice, but Anarigar hesitated to say as much. He knew the girl would be insulted, and she would sulk for the rest of the trip.

"Maybe it is best if you don't sing. The drometarius needs to be able to listen for any threat. I suspect the animal was confused when it could not hear the desert sounds above your singing."

"Oh, I never thought of that. I was just bored, and I wanted to make the trip more fun. I guess the drometarius needs to be able to hear even the slightest noises if it is going to protect us, right?" Nalivia said innocently, completely unaware that she had been insulted.

"I think that is best. Stay as quiet as you can. In fact, I just lean back on my drometarius' hump and take a nap. It will help make the time pass by faster if you do the same," Anarigar suggested.

Smiling to himself, Anarigar returned to his own drometarius. However, Anarigar was unable to allow himself to fall back to sleep. He rode through the heat of the day without closing his eyes.

As evening approached, Anarigar halted his drometarius and suggested setting up camp. Building a fire from dried dung, Anarigar cooked two portions of food for himself and Nalivia. Nalivia knew better than to ask what he was cooking. She was warned that she would be eating lizard at some point on the trip and did not want to know if it would be tonight. The longer she could pretend it was chicken or some desert grouse, the happier she would be.

Anarigar seemed unwilling to spend time after dinner in conversation. He said he needed to take care of the drometarius, set up the tents, and many other chores. He suggested Nalivia wipe the dishes with sand to clean them.

Nalivia thought it was unsanitary to wash the pots used for cooking with sand, but she knew water was scarce, and it could not be wasted. Rowanda told her many tales of her time spent in the desert, so she was not surprised when asked to use the sand. She went about the task and found it was easier than using soap and water. A quick wipe with a cloth to get the residue off the utensils and pots and the dishes were done. A smile crossed her face when she accomplished the task in less than two minutes.

Sitting near the fire, Nalivia thought about singing to keep herself amused, and then she remembered she must be silent so the drometarius could hear if a creature were sneaking towards them. With a loud sigh, Nalivia sat and started to let herself feel grumpy. She imagined Rowanda was having a much grander time with Emeraza and Beir as company. When Anarigar returned, he set up her tent first so that she could go in and sleep.

"Don't you want to sit and look at the stars with me for a while before we go to sleep?" Nalivia asked coquettishly. She was fascinated with the older boy and daydreamed about marrying him one day.

"I see the stars every night. I think it would be better if we both got a good night's sleep. We have another long day of travel tomorrow. I do have one question before we go to sleep. Do you have a weapon with you in case we encounter terpor or wetchels? The drometarius will let us know, but I may need a bit of help fighting one if it would come to that."

Nalivia took a mental inventory of her charms. She had little practice with them before having to leave with Emeraza, Rowanda, and Beir. She knew when Rowanda first came to Arolsen, she had no training with her charms, and yet she could use them.

"I can start a fire, which I can control well enough to aim at a target. I am not sure exactly how my other charms can be used for protection yet, but if the threat arises, I will find out. I suspect I would be able to cause a sandstorm or cyclone much as Rowanda did when she was here before, but...I don't know for sure. Let's just hope nothing tries to attack us." Nalivia said as she got to her feet.

Going into her small tent, Nalivia sat upon the cushion provided and looked at her charms. They were an odd assortment, but Emeraza said the crystalized teardrop, in particular, was unique and special. Nalivia didn't know how she was supposed to use it. It represented Water, but what form would it take. Could she use it in conjunction with her hand trowel to grow plants as Rowanda did with her chalice and pouch of seeds? Maybe the teardrop could find water or yet, perhaps it could cause rain or hail or possibly even a flood. She wished more than ever that she would have trained longer before coming to Arolsen. How could any of the charms help her to find talisman here?

The next morning, Anarigar called for her to get up and get ready for breakfast. He had once again fixed something in the pot, but this time there was no meat. It tasted much like oatmeal. Nalivia ate it and complimented the cook.

Anarigar seemed not to be flattered. He ate and said nothing. Taking the pot, he cleaned it out with sand and waited for Nalivia to finish. Anarigar packed up the tents with the cushions rolled up inside, and he strapped them to the drometarius. He was ready to mount when Nalivia pointed in the distance and asked what was making the sand fly.

Both drometarius started to complain. "Mount up quickly, Nalivia. We are going to try to outrun the terpor!" Anarigar shouted.

Barely having time to get into place, the drometarius rose and broke into another gallop staying close on his companion's heels. Nalivia felt as though she was banging back and forth, like a gong in a bell, between the two humps. Being battered in the process, fear kept her focused on holding on and not complaining.

Anarigar kept looking back to see if the terpor was getting closer. Giving his drometarius another incentive to run faster, Anarigar batted his rump. The animal moved out at an even higher speed, putting some distance between himself and Nalivia's drometarius. Not wanting to be separated, Nalivia's drometarius pushed himself to keep pace.

The sand drifts flew past the two running animals, and Nalivia found it more difficult to breathe as the wind swept past her mouth and nostrils. The sand being flung up from the flying feet of the drometarius stung Nalivia's face, and she wished she took the time to secure her cloak around her head to protect herself before leaving.

Anarigar's drometarius started to slow. Nalivia was unsure if the terpor had given up the chase or if the drometarius was exhausted. As her own drometarius came alongside Anarigar's drometarius, Nalivia asked. "Did we lose the terpor, or is your drometarius just too tired to keep running?"

"I think the terpor gave up. I don't see any signs of shifting sand, which indicates the movement of the terpor under the sand. We can slow down and let the drometarius rest, but I will keep watch to make sure the serpent is not creeping up onto us." Anarigar looked wary as he spoke to Nalivia.

"What weapon do you carry to protect yourself?" Nalivia asked, suddenly being aware of her own safety.

Anarigar patted his pack. I have a sword, lance, and my leather-covered longbow with wooden arrows. I also carry a knife strapped to my forearm. I would rather not let a terpor get close enough to use my sword. I am very good with my bow and arrows, but many of the larger terpor are unaffected by the arrows even with fixed blade broadheads unless one hits the creature in the eye. It is not easy to hit a terpor in the eye while riding on a galloping drometarius. My father can, though."

Nalivia thought about her hand trowel and how it could possibly be used to protect her from a terpor. She hoped she would not need to find out if it was useless against a terpor any time soon.

Anarigar pointed towards the mountain. With their attention focused on pursuing terpor, neither of the two travelers had realized how close they were getting to their destination.

Nalivia could see why the mountain was described as a horned lizard. The rolling peaks jutted out in places giving one the impression that at any moment, the mountain could take to its legs and run across the desert floor like a fleeing lizard. Nalivia was enjoying her moment of fantasy when Anarigar broke the silence.

"We will make camp at the bottom of the mountain tonight. Tomorrow morning, we will decide whether we will need to climb or if there will be an opening for us to use to go into the belly of the mountain," Anarigar said quietly. "It is a sacred mountain. I am not sure what will be allowed. My grandfather said that ancient kings were buried here, and their spirits guard their burial site. I do not want to offend them."

Nalivia did not comment. She was unsure what her role was except to find charms from Arolsen that Boultori could use instead of using Rowanda's charms. No one told her where to go to seek for the charms. She was just told that her own talismans would guide her. Here she and Anarigar were on the mountain, and she felt nothing from her charms. She wondered if the mountain was a mistake, and maybe they should have gone another direction. She would need to wait until the morning to find out.

Nalivia slept fitfully at the base of the mountain. She wondered if terpor lived in the sandstone. Possibly, they could tunnel through the rock. Maybe they were the guardians of the ancient kings. Nalivia didn't want to find out if her charms could stop a terpor. She didn't want to find out if Anarigar could shoot an arrow into a terpor's eye, either. She sure did not wish to have a terpor close enough that Anarigar would need to use a lance or sword. Nightmares woke her when she would drift off to sleep.

Anarigar woke her when Nalivia finally fell asleep. She woke up and rubbed her eyes. Sand had irritated them as they fled the terpor, and her eyes were burning and felt raw. Her clothes were scratchy from grains of sand that clung to her skin. All in all, Nalivia was not in a good mood.

Walking out from her tent, Anarigar announced that the camp would remain on this ground, and the drometarius would be hobbled. Anarigar had explored as Nalivia slept.

"I have found a narrow opening between the walls of the mountain. It is wide enough to allow us to pass, but I don't want to take the drometarius. It would be difficult for them to turn around in such a tight space. We will have no trouble. I have packed water and some food, even though we will probably only spend a few hours in this canyon. Here is some hardtack for you to eat. I want to go before it gets hot," Anarigar said as he handed Nalivia the hard bread.

Nalivia took the hardtack and munched on it, aware it would cause her to be thirsty. Even before needing to ask, Anarigar handed her a flask of water.

They walked along the narrow canyon with tall walls on either side of them, not knowing how far the canyon would take them. Looking up along both sides of the wall, Nalivia saw striations of color as sand had settled, forming the rock from ages ago.

Following Anarigar for hours, sipping on water when her tongue felt as though it was swelling, Nalivia was surprised by Anarigar's sudden halt.

"It's a dead-end," Anarigar said disappointedly. "I don't know what I was hoping for, but not for a dead end."

Anarigar started to turn around when Nalivia grabbed his sleeve. "Wait, I see a crack in the wall. I want to check it out."

Nalivia walked to the crack and felt it. Taking her hand trowel from her belt, she started to scrape at the opening.

Anarigar watched, hoping the spirits would not be offended by the noise Nalivia was making when suddenly, a sharp breaking sound was heard, and rocks begin to cascade through the crack. The crack became larger and larger as more rocks crumbled to the ground.

"Stop! I think you are waking the spirits!" Anarigar said as he pulled Nalivia from her work.

"No, wait, Anarigar. I am not doing the digging. It is my hand trowel doing all the work. I am just holding on to it. It is doing all the digging by itself. I think this is the sign for which Emeraza said to watch."

Anarigar released Nalivia and stood back as her hand trowel worked at a speed impossible for any human. Nalivia stood as if in a trance and allowed her arm to work furiously to dig the hole large enough for her and Anarigar to pass within.

When the hole was completed, the hand trowel stopped its activities. Nalivia's arm dropped to her side. Putting the tool back into her belt, Nalivia shook her arm to let blood to flow freely again.

"That was weird. My arm is absolutely numb," Nalivia announced.

Stepping into the hole, Nalivia said she wished they had a light source. "It is really dark in here."

Just as she said those words out loud, she giggled. "Silly me, I have a piece of coal."

"Great! What good is a piece of coal," said Anarigar thinking Nalivia was truly as childish as he had surmised her to be.

"Watch," Nalivia said as she took the coal out of her pouch. A small flame ignited, which spread light within the cavern they had just entered.

"Aieee! Isn't that burning your hand?" Anarigar said as he saw the flame sitting on Nalivia's palm.

"Not at all," Nalivia remarked, looking rather proud of herself. "Keep close. We need to see what is inside. I know now this is where we are supposed to be. Help me keep an eye out for charms."

Anarigar looked around the cavern. "Give me some ideas. What should I expect to see?"

"I don't know. The charms could be anything. My charms are the hand trowel I used to get into this cavern, the coal that is lighting the way, a bumblebee's wing, which I have no idea how to use, and my crystalized teardrop. Look for anything normal or out of the norm, for that matter."

"You sure make it easy for a guy," Anarigar said sarcastically.

Walking more in-depth into the cavern, Nalivia stopped and looked down at her feet. "What do you suppose that might be?"

Anarigar picked up the object and inspected it more closely. "It is a piece of bone. I think it might be a bone from a finger."

"Hang onto it. It just might be a charm. We will need to find as many as possible since I have no idea which charm may pick Boultori. He will need many to choose from before four chooses him."

"That doesn't even make any sense. Boultori needs many to choose from so four can choose him?" Anarigar said as he placed the bone inside a pocket within his robe.

"Aww, look! See how that stone sparkles in the light. I think we should take it, too. Many charms are crystals or gems." Nalivia picked it up and said with glee, "It is blue. I know this is special. Here, put it with the bone."

Anarigar was starting to enjoy the search for charms. It was like a treasure hunt. Scurrying in front of Nalivia, he bent down and forced a petrified bat into her face.

Screeching, Nalivia screamed, "Yikes! That is icky. Take that thing out of my face. It gives me the creeps. That is just ugly. Put it in your pocket, and don't put it in my face again!"

Anarigar laughed. This was the first time he enjoyed being in Nalivia's company. She was like having a little sister that he could tease. Anarigar kept his eyes peeled for another object that might cause the same reaction.

A few minutes passed with nothing happening of interest. Nalivia knew that ordinary items could become charms. "Hey, I have an idea. I will put the coal away, so there is no light and see if anything calls out to me."

"I don't think that is a good idea. I really don't want to be in this cavern without light. Remember, we are trespassing on sacred grounds. If anything comes out to meet us, I want to be able to see it. I don't like your...."

Nalivia put her piece of coal back into her pouch just as Anarigar was about to say 'idea.' Expecting the cavern to be pitch black, Nalivia was delighted to find the cavern gleamed and glittered.

"Ah, it is beautiful. It is like being in the desert night with millions of stars twinkling up in the sky. Anarigar! Look how wonderful it is. No wonder your spirits want to be here. It is magical!"

Turning slowly in place, Anarigar was looking in wonder as well. He was too speechless to say anything about how incredible it was until he saw two eyes staring at him.

Grabbing Nalivia, he said, "Run!"

CHAPTER NINE

 Salitha, Alfinia, Scherra, and Iona, four of Neslora's elders, were left with the duty to train the remaining young apprentices as well as dividing into two groups with the townsmen who would be stationed at the two possible confluences Salitha identified in her dream. Each traveling sorceress would take two or three apprentices. Two sorceresses would remain in the village. Emeraza, before leaving for Arolsen, asked the remaining two sorceresses to start the search for prospective apprentices from amongst the younger girls. It would be a difficult task as the traits would not be as identifiable at such a young age. It was decided Scherra would remain with Iona at the village as both elders were ancient, and travel would be particularly hard on them.

Salitha drew a map, and Alfinia, with many townsmen, Opaline, Estella and Thaliana was assigned the closest of the two confluences from Salitha's dream. Salitha knew the confluence where the ground was burned out, and several abductions had previously taken place, was closed for good, so it did not need to be guarded. On Emeraza's orders, Salitha permanently closed the opening behind Emeraza, Beir, Rowanda, and Nalivia. Emeraza wanted no chance of the Arolsen men entering again through the previous confluence that was so close to the village.

In the mirrored worlds, the palace city of Arolsen is found in the north. The main village of Neslora, on the other world, is located in the south. The new confluences in Salitha dreams are expected to be used by the king's men to return to Neslora. Salitha and her entourage are heading there to intercept them.

Every preparation was made for the trip, and for the many days or weeks, the party would be camped at those two places. The men of the village met before leaving. Plans were drawn up for traps to capture anyone who might step upon their land from Arolsen. That meant tools would need to be used to dig deep pits, and large nets were also placed in the wagons that would carry all the items to the destinations.

The girls had the option of riding in one of the wagons but chose to run alongside the cart at the start. Each girl was excited to be able to leave the village and not be under the watchful eyes of their mothers. They knew their fathers would be too busy building traps to oversee them. Each thought they would have time to play.

Magdelan and Breanna were assigned to Salitha. They knew Salitha to be a gentlewoman. They could not imagine her scolding them for any reason. Their misunderstanding of how dire the circumstances may be, caused them to have a frivolous attitude, which Salitha knew she would need to correct.

"Girls, this is not a holiday. This is very serious. Both of your mothers were amongst the women who were abducted. Just because Rowanda rescued them quickly, does not mean that it won't happen again. This time it could be you forced into the service of the king of Arolsen. Imagine your life as a slave.... Now, I want both of you to get serious about your training and what we will need to do when we reach the place where soldiers of Arolsen will enter. I repeat, will enter, not might enter!" Salitha stared at the two girls watching as their smiles evaporated from their faces.

Salitha added, "I think skipping along beside the wagon is a good idea. Both of you seem to have too much energy at the moment.

Maybe with tired muscles, your mind might be able to grasp the severity of the situation."

Salitha knew she had just made their fun into a punishment. As she was helped into the wagon, a smile crossed her face. She just proved she could be assertive when she needed to be.

The ride did not seem very long since Salitha's mind was preoccupied with planning. Tents would be erected, and meal planning was necessary as well. Two women volunteered to come and prepare meals for the men, Salitha, and the two apprentices. The two women having no talents with sorcery, felt it was their duty to help as they were able. Their children's lives could be at stake.

Salitha's tent would also house the two girls. While their tents were being erected, Salitha called the girls to her for a lesson. Asking each girl to show her the charms that had chosen them, Salitha decided to begin her instructions regarding the responsibilities of having charms, as well as the safety factors.

Taking the girls further away from the campsite, Salitha took out one of her own charms. Targeting a bright orange flower, a known favorite of all the people of Neslora, Salitha pointed her talisman at the bloom and withered it within seconds.

A gasp broke from both of the girl's mouths. "Elder, that was awful. Why did you destroy that beautiful flower?" Breanna asked sadly.

"You both have the power of great destruction, but as sorceresses of Neslora, your power should only be used for the good of our world and its people. I wanted to show you how devastating our charms can be if misused."

Taking a second charm from her pouch, Salitha once again pointed the talisman towards the dead bloom. With a flick of her wrist and a soft word spoken, the dead flower slowly softened and became pliable. A touch of salmon color returned to the bloom as it started to thrive. Reaching its full glory once again, the muted orange coloring became vibrant.

"Now, let me see your charms. Lay them at your feet," Salitha instructed.

Taking inventory of each girl's charms, Salitha asked the girls to pick the one that represented Water. Neither girl was sure which one it might be. Neither had a piece of coral, river rock, or an apparent water charm.

"Look closely at your charms. What do you see? Remember that Rowanda's Water charm was a chalice, and Nalivia's Water charm was her own tear. You need to recognize what Water may mean to you."

Breanna was the first to show a sign of understanding. "I think I know my talisman that represents water. I think this feather is from a swan. Am I correct?"

Salitha smiled to show her pleasure. "That is absolutely correct. That is a swan's feather. Not all charms will be obvious. The swan is dependent upon water for its survival; therefore, its feather represents water."

Magdelan's face showed a new understanding. "I know which one of my charms represents the element Water. It is this sea green colored triangle. The triangle represents water, right?"

"Yes, Magdelan, you are right. The sea green color was a giveaway even if you did not know that the shape was the symbol of water. Very good, both of you. Now, let us practice using our charms to make water appear."

The lessons continued until the three were called to dinner. Salitha decided any further lessons could wait in the morning as the girls were tired from running along beside the wagon for many miles. The morning would bring work for all. Supervising the men at work, while also instructing the apprentices would make for a hectic day for Salitha. A good night's sleep would benefit them all.

The birds chirping woke Salitha. She put aside her sleeping gown and put on her clothing. She let the girls sleep as she walked out into the fresh morning air. Several of the men were up drinking a warm beverage the two women had prepared first thing in the morning. Salitha could smell the aroma of food cooking over the campfire. Walking towards Paol, the foreman in charge of the work detail was greeted by Salitha with a smile.

"Good morning, Paol. I am impressed that you and your men are up so early and ready to work. Much depends on the preparation at this site. My dream showed a confluence at exactly the spot you are standing on at this very moment."

Startled, Paol stepped aside from where he was standing. "This very spot, Elder?"

Salitha came forward and placed a large stick, poking it into the ground. "This very spot. I am suggesting that your men dig a huge pit exactly where the stick indicates. As the king's men enter into our world, they will fall into the pit, and we can capture them. I don't think they will be expecting a trap."

"Yes, Elder. I will begin the task immediately after breakfast. Depending on how deep and wide you would like the pit, we could probably have it completed by mid-afternoon. Will you want to inspect it before we camouflage the opening?" Paol said, expecting an answer.

"I will come by after the noon meal to see how things are progressing. I know my two apprentices will want a break from my prattle by then," Salitha said with a wink.

"You never prattle, Elder Salitha," Paol said with reverence.

Turning to make sure her two students were awake, dressed, and eating breakfast before the morning lessons, Salitha was found wandering amongst the men who came to protect Neslora. Salitha greeted each and every one of them, complimenting them on their determination to keep Neslora a safe place for their children and grandchildren.

Respectfully, the men answered the elder's comments, questions, and good-natured joking. The two young ladies noticed how much love and esteem Salitha commanded from the sturdy men and realized she was not the silly old woman they had assumed her to be. Just because Elder Salitha did not scare them to death the way Emeraza could, did not mean she was a toothless old hag, not worthy of esteem. Both girls felt ashamed knowing they had often laughed at her behind her back.

As Salitha approached the two girls, both jumped to their feet to show respect. "Girls, sit down and finish your breakfast. We will begin our studies soon enough. I think you have time for a cup of tea as well."

Salitha joined the two women who had prepared the breakfast for all the campers. She talked in a low voice with them and enjoyed a plate of food. Soon, the two women were gathering dishes to clean, and Salitha knew it was time to start the lessons.

Finding a soft spot under a tree, Salitha placed a blanket on the grass for the girls to sit upon. The lesson the evening before was introducing the charms to each student. They were to think about their charms, talk to them, and sleep with them. This morning, Salitha hoped to go beyond introductions and to use each one separately and then in combinations. Realizing for some of the charms to be used, they must move further from where the men were working. Accidents often happen at the beginning of lessons involving charms. There was no sense of burning down the tents or accidentally injuring one of the men.

Picking up the blanket, Salitha asked the girls to follow her further into the woods. Once she had gone a kilometer away, Salitha decided it was probably safe to begin.

Asking the girls to find the talismans that represented Fire, they would begin by focusing their charms at the small brook flowing through the trees.

"This area of the brook is low, and almost no fish ever come this far for fear of getting stuck in the shallow water where they could become stranded. I think it is safe to aim your charms at this part of the brook. If you are careful not to start a forest fire, I think we can begin," Salitha instructed.

Magdelan and Breanna reached into their pouches and gently picked up the talisman that represented Fire. Standing a meter apart or more, as suggested by Salitha, the two girls concentrated on a rock in the middle of the stream.

"Before unleashing your flame, could either of you tell me if fire can ricochet? I see you have both chosen to aim your talisman at a rock," Salitha said, not adding another word.

"Therefore, you are saying that blaze can glance off the rock and maybe start a fire in the trees or burn the grass on the other side of the stream?" Magdelan asked.

Salitha looked towards Breanna to answer the question. "What do you think, Breanna? Is it possible that aiming one's charm at one thing could possibly cause a hazard somewhere else you may not have anticipated?"

Breanna looked at her, Elder, "Why yes, Elder. If my flame should hit a hard object, it could be deflected at an angle and then hit a soft object where the flame would spread. I think if Magdelan and I aim at the water and not at the rocks in the water, we may be safer."

"That is totally correct," Salitha commended the young girl. "I know you have not been taught physics or geometry yet, so I am proud that you understand the theory and practice of trajectory."

Breanna beamed at Salitha's high praise. She held her charm at arm's length, making sure there were no rocks in the stream when she allowed herself to think fire.

A flashing blaze erupted from her charm, and Magdelan watched as steam hissed from the stream. "You did it, Breanna. Let me try."

Magdelan pointed her talisman in the same general direction and was pleased when she produced a steady blaze of fire. Taking their complete concentration, neither girl could sustain the flame for any length of time.

Salitha changed the subject to the talisman that controlled Air to allow the girls' brains to focus on a new task and to let what they had just learned sink in. The time passed quickly as the two apprentices were thrilled with their new-found powers. Salitha realized it was past time for the noon meal, so she told the girls it was time to break.

"Oh, do we have to..." whined Breanna. "I am really enjoying learning everything that I can do with my charms. I am not hungry. Let's keep practicing."

"Come on, girls. I need to see how the men have progressed with the pit they are digging. I told Paol that I would return to inspect the work they have done. I never go back on my word. We will continue after our light meal," Salitha said as she gathered the blanket and shooed the girls towards the camp.

Gleefully, the two scampered off ahead of Salitha. Running forward, they were out of sight in no time. Their giggles let Salitha know just how far they might be. She followed the path back to the camp.

Seeing the men breaking for lunch and a rest, Salitha walked over to the pit. She was aghast. Sharpened spears were placed in the pit with the sharpened point reaching up towards the sky.

"Paol! We want to trap and capture the men from Arolsen, not kill them! We are not hunting tigers or bears. These are humans. Many of them are not here by their own choice but because the king has commanded them to come," Salitha scolded.

"These men abducted our women. They will not get a chance to do that again," Paol stated.

"I command that you take those spears out of the pit. We will be placing leaves to break their fall. I do not want a single man to be hurt!" Salitha did not look back but stomped away to where the two women were preparing her dish.

"My, my, my," Salitha said while shaking her head in disbelief. "I know our men are warriors, and they think the people of Arolsen are our enemies, but I didn't expect such savagery."

One of the women handed Salitha a dish of food. "I will talk to Paol. My sister was one of the women abducted along with your daughter. She told me the guards were never cruel to them. In fact, she told me the guards often brought extra blankets and food even when the king said the women should have nothing since they failed to produce plants. I think once he hears how nice the guards were, he may start to share your idea of capturing the men from Arolsen without harming them."

Salitha patted the woman's hand. "Thank you, dear, for offering to talk to Paol. I am sure it could not harm the situation, and it may smooth it over a bit. He seems a little annoyed at my suggestion to remove the sharpened pikes."

Salitha was hoping the pit being dug where the other confluence would appear, would not have sharped pikes either. She could not worry about what was happening elsewhere. That was Elder Alfinia's problem. Alfinia was petty and irritable, but she was not stupid. She would know how to handle most issues that might arise.

CHAPTER TEN

The morning sun had barely entered the small slit in the prison wall when guards came to make sure Boultori was awake and ready for another day's work planting crops for his brother's delight. A meager breakfast was pushed into the cell, and the guard apologized for the small portion.

"I am sorry, My lord. Your brother is watching to make sure no one gives you more than he has said you should have. If it were up to me, I would triple the amount on your plate and make sure you had honey for your dried bread. Sadly, it is not up to me," the guard said in a hushed tone.

The guard continued talking, sounding almost like Boultori's mother, "Eat while you can. I am to have you in the field before the morning sky's color turns to blue. Right now, the pink tint is giving way to the bright, scorching sun. I fear it is going to be a sweltering day. Make sure to cover your head before we leave."

Boultori knew the guard was forced into his brother's army. Many of the men worked for fear their families would be punished if they did not comply. King Nashua was not a popular king, but he was powerful. Being a wizard and an evil wizard, at that, made him dreaded. Once a company of guards had revolted and attempted to overthrow the king. They were met by crushing stones cast upon them by the king. None survived the onslaught. No soldier was brave enough to attempt a coup again.

Trudging out of the palace under guard. The guards removed Boultori's chains to free him for his work. Boultori was given Rowanda's chalice and a pouch of seeds. King Nashua kept the items under lock and key when not being used by Boultori.

Boultori now viewed the two charms as contemptible. What Boultori once saw as a miraculous solution to the desolation of Arolsen, had become his life sentence. Boultori, however, was not morose. He was not one to accept his fate. He would find a way out.

Listening to every word the guards said as he toiled day after day, Boultori was thinking of a plan for escape. One guard said that today was the day the king planned to send guards into Neslora to capture slaves to work his gardens and crops.

"It seems the king has finally realized that the men and women of the palace city know little about crops or gardens. King Nashua is sending troops from the palace garrison into Neslora at two separate confluences to bring back slaves. That will be good for my sister, who tires of working long days in the hot sun to prune bushes. I know your son is tired of digging irrigation ditches to bring water to the crops. I do feel sorry for the abducted people of Neslora. Working for King Nashua is going to be a rude awakening from the life they have been living in their world."

Boultori, still listening, heard the response from the other guard saying, "I know one confluence will be close by. I heard the King ranting about his original confluence no longer responding to his magic. With a smirk, the king said he would just open another or maybe even two to take the people of Neslora totally by surprise. From what I understand, twenty guards will enter at each point. Happily, I won't be one of them. Have you heard yet whether you will need to go?"

The first guard responded, "Yes, I am one of the unlucky ones who will be going. In fact, I see the other guards gathering now. I don't think you will need a replacement guard as Boultori is a model prisoner. Right, Boultori?"

"Boultori never lifted his head from his work. "That is right, Boss. You know I am nothing but an old fool."

"Well, I must join the ranks. I sure don't want the wizard to see me slacking. I don't want to end up on the end of a rope or worse," said the first guard as he walked to join the other soldiers about to leave for the confluence.

Boultori took a single seed from his pouch and dropped it into a small hole he had made with his toe. Pouring water from the chalice, a vine rapidly grew with tendrils growing out like fingers. Knocking his guard on the head with the grail, Boultori quickly stripped the man of his outer garments. Putting them on rapidly, Boultori knew he could now pass as one of the king's guards. With a quick command to the plant to wrap around the guard to secure him, Boultori was at the end of the troops marching towards his means of escape.

Staying at the end of the line of soldiers, Boultori followed in step as best as he could. Never having drilled in the art of marching, Boultori missed a step or two but regained his cadence quickly. Having his head covered except for his eyes, Boultori was sure no one would give him a second look as they continued their march.

When the commander put up his hand to signal a halt, Boultori realized for the first time that his brother was at the head of the marching men on his favorite dapple-gray stallion. Boultori knew he would need to keep his distance.

King Nashua remained on his steed. "Today, you are favored. You have been tasked to bring back slaves from Neslora to tend my gardens and crops. Each of you will be awarded a basket of fruit, grain, and vegetables from my own crops. I will open the confluence so you can enter, and on the second day, I will open the confluence for you to bring your prisoners to our land. Two days should be sufficient for you to gather the number of slaves I will require. Be back to the confluence on the designated day...with slaves, or you will forfeit a family member each. Do not try to escape in Neslora or someone you love will die. Now, on a happy note, go and serve the king as I have commanded."

King Nashua waved his wand, and an opening began to appear. At first, it looked like a desert mirage with wavering lines in the sky. As the opening widened, a lush green world could be seen through the hole. Birds could be heard chirping and trees swayed gently in the fresh, clean air. The color was scattered everywhere. One soldier could be heard audibly gasping.

"Remember your loved ones..." were the King's final words as each soldier entered Neslora until the opening behind them closed with a flash of light and a crackle of air.

Forming into a line, two-by-two, the soldiers started to march but found themselves falling into a deep pit upon entering Neslora. The first few men landed with a thud, and each man after that fell heavily on top of the first several. Moans and cries of pain could be heard when all, but the last five men came tumbling down.

The last five men stopped quickly and managed not to fall. Immediately, they were surrounded by men from Neslora and were told to get on their knees and put their hands behind their backs. Each did as they were told and found themselves being bound and dragged, chained together under a tree to await their companions' retrieval from the pit.

Boultori watched as more soldiers from Neslora came from bushes to lend a hand, as every man from Arolsen was pulled out of the pit, chained and placed with the other captured men. When the last man was finally removed from the pit, a tall man asked who was in charge.

The second in command of the king's guard yelled, "That would be me."

Paol walked up to the man and stood him on his feet. "We know you have been sent to our world to capture slaves to work in your king's gardens and cropland. You will not find any slaves here. In fact, you have two choices. You may stay in Neslora and become a citizen, or you may return to Arolsen and meet your fate at your king's hand."

The mumbling became loud as each man was whispering their fears for their loved ones at the same time. Finally, one brave man asked to speak. "Sir, if we do not return with slaves, our family members will be killed."

"If you return without slaves, will your loved ones be spared?" Paol asked calmly.

No one spoke. Each knew that the possibility of family members being killed was a probability. The king did not accept failure. When he commanded something, his subjects had only one choice, and that was to do exactly as ordered.

Paol watched as grown men started to cry. Each was thinking of a wife, a child, a sibling, a mother, or a father who would pay with their life because of their failure.

Boultori had remained silent and in the background until this moment. Struggling to get to his feet, he asked if his hands could be untied.

"Why would I untie your hands?" Paol asked amusedly.

One of the guards gasped, "He is the king's brother. That man is Boultori!"

Paol knew nothing of Boultori. He was about to say that it was good to have a bargaining chip when Salitha came forward from where she was standing with her two young apprentices.

"Paol, bring Boultori to me," Salitha said quietly but in a stern voice. "I wish to talk with the king's brother."

Boultori was unchained from the others and was brought to Salitha. She indicated that Boultori should be brought to her tent. Untying Boultori's hand, she asked Magdelan to retrieve a cup of tea for her guest and dismissed both girls from her tent.

"Sit, please," Salitha said, indicating a camping cot for him to sit upon. "I am afraid I have nothing more comfortable for you to sit upon as we are camping out here."

Boultori sat where Salitha indicated. "Now, please tell me what you know. I believe you are friends with my son-in-law, Beirimor."

A smile broke across Boultori's face. "Is Beir here? I want to see him as soon as I can. I have brought Rowanda's chalice and the pouch of seeds with me."

"Oh, my," Salitha said with a frown. "I am afraid that Beir, Rowanda, and Emeraza are in Arolsen trying to find you at this very moment."

Boultori was visibly shaken. "Beir and Rowanda came back to Arolsen to find me? Can you get word to them to return immediately to Neslora?"

"I am afraid we have no way to communicate through the confluence. They are searching for you in Arolsen, and here you are in Neslora. I am afraid that the only solution will be for you to return to Arolsen to find them. Rowanda has need of her chalice and pouch of seeds. I fear I must task you with their return."

"Can you open the confluence?" Boultori asked Salitha.

"I am an Elder, and even though my powers are not as great as they once were when I was young, I can indeed manage a charm or two. I can open the confluence, but the question is, when will it be safe? Does your king have guards waiting on the other side?" Salitha asked.

Boultori puzzled a few moments, thinking. "The king is an arrogant man. I don't think he would think that he would need to leave guards. I guess that his guards escorted him back to the palace. The plan was to leave the twenty guards in Neslora for two days to gather slaves and then return to this exact spot where the king will open the confluence and receive his new workers. If you could open the confluence tonight, I could slip back into Arolsen and find Beir and Rowanda and whoever Emeraza might be. Can you give me any details as to where they entered Arolsen?"

When the tea arrived, the two sat down to make plans. Salitha told Boultori that the three of the travelers had entered Arolsen, where Rowanda first came through, but that confluence was now permanently closed.

"There is another confluence that King Nashua plans to open tomorrow for more soldiers to enter Neslora," Boultori said, offering information.

"I am very aware of the other site. I have men stationed there along with another sorceress and her three apprentices. They will encounter the same fate as your traveling companions," Salitha said with a wink.

"How is it that you knew we would be coming and when?" Boultori asked.

Salitha offered, "The when was not known but the where I saw in my dream. I had a feeling we had very little time to prepare, so that is why you have found us camped at this site."

Boultori chuckled. "I don't know if it was a good thing or a bad thing that I managed to escape and tag along with this group of soldiers. I only hope it is a good thing in the long run. I pray Beir and Rowanda do not go to the palace to try to rescue me. I suspect the first place they headed for was Beir's and my oasis. If so, Beir would discover that I never came home. I am sure he would have heard rumors of my being held prisoner by my brother. Knowing

Beir and Rowanda, they would head straight to the palace. Is Emeraza more sensible than my old friends?"

Now Salitha chuckled, "Emeraza is considered wise being The Elder, but between you and me, she lacks all sense when it comes to her son. The years she thought him dead hardened her to the point of pragmatism. She was logical, and without compassion, some said. Now that her son has returned, I have seen her heart soften again. I am not sure she will stop and think as she once did but follow her son's instincts without question. I rather think Rowanda will be the one who is rational if Beir is not."

"The Little Dragon? Rational? You do know that child is without fear. She challenged a terpor! She is a menace." Boultori said, standing up, knocking over his tea.

"That menace is my granddaughter!" Salitha said bristling.

Sensing Salitha irritation, Boultori quickly added, "Don't get me wrong. I meant menace in the most loving words imaginable. The Little Dragon stole my heart. I would do anything for her. She gave me her chalice and pouch of seeds to make my world better. She is like a daughter to me. I meant no disrespect, but if you think Rowanda is sensible, I will need to debate you. She is brave, kind, but rash. I just don't want to think about my brother capturing her. It would be horrible for her...."

Salitha knew time was not on their side. "I will open the confluence as soon as it is dark. You will slip in, and I will close it on your heels. It is imperative that you find Rowanda and return the chalice and seeds. Her full powers will be needed for Emeraza and Rowanda to overthrow your brother. The plan is for Nalivia to find an assortment of charms from your world that you will be able to use to help your people once your brother is no longer king. With your charms, you will be able to take your brother's place on the throne and make Arolsen a better place for all your people. Rowanda said you are a kind man, and that is all that you have ever wanted. She wants to help you to succeed."

"Who is Nalivia? You never mentioned four people entered Arolsen.

"Nalivia is another apprentice. She is untried as was Rowanda when she first entered Arolsen, but Nalivia's charms are a strange and odd assortment that made her the perfect choice to accompany the others. Her task, as I said, is to find the charms that will choose you. I don't know where she is or when she will meet with Emeraza, Beir, and Rowanda, but if you find those three, you will soon have charms from your world that will assist you in becoming the King of Arolsen."

Boultori sat meditatively. Salitha stepped out of her tent long enough to ask the two girls to bring food for her guest. When she returned to her tent, Boultori said without a hint of humor. "We have another problem. The soldiers who came to Neslora did not come on their own accord. The king has forced them to find slaves. If they do not succeed, their family members will be killed. You can't let that happen. You must think of a way so that their families will not be harmed."

Salitha said, "I will spend my time thinking about how we can make sure the families of these men will not be harmed. I will ask for the guidance of the men who came with me. All are great warriors, but they are all also family men. They are not without compassion. We will think of something. Your job is to return and find Rowanda. Let me do what I can from here to help your men."

As evening approached, Salitha brought Boultori out of her tent. "It is time for you to return to Arolsen and find Rowanda. It is imperative that you reunite Rowanda with her two missing charms. You must not be caught by your brother. He may have posted a guard at the confluence, so be careful. It is time for me to reopen the confluence. Are you ready?"

Boultori nodded and walked beside Salitha as she took out her charms. Holding all four of her talismans, Salitha muttered some words that Boultori could not understand. A sparkling light, not unlike a firefly, twinkled in the air before him. As it widened, Boultori could see the evening sky from Arolsen starting to appear.

"Move through quickly. I will not allow the confluence to stay open longer than what it takes for you to step through," Salitha warned.

Without a backward glance, Boultori stepped through, hoping there would be no guard to impede his way. With a snap, the confluence closed behind him. Seeing no guard, Boultori made haste to leave the sight. Which direction he would ultimately go was not a concern at the moment. Boultori wanted to get as far away from this part of the desert as he could.

Seeing a cloud of dust surrounding the palace walls, Boultori knew many guards were searching for him. Boultori was sure his brother was informed of his escape. There was no way Boultori would be able to return to the palace city without being seen.

Making a wide detour, Boultori decided to head to the oasis to see if, by chance, Beir was there. Getting supplies from his sanctuary was a second reason to choose that direction as a starting place for his search.

Walking all night long at a fast pace and part of the next day, found Boultori nearing his oasis. The first thing Boultori noticed was the absence of the livestock. It was unrealistic to think Anarigar would have remained at the oasis all this time.

Going into his tent, Boultori dropped to the pillows. He would take a nap before collecting his gear. Returning to the palace city was probably the most sensible plan of action. Boultori reasoned that Beir would assume that he was being held a prisoner. Right now, sleep was what Boultori needed most.

CHAPTER ELEVEN

 Anarigar screamed, "Run!" again, as he grabbed Nalivia's hand and pulled her towards the opening she created in the cavern. Pulling against Anarigar's hand, Nalivia slipped free and stopped running.

"We need to see what those eyes belong to, Anarigar. Arm yourself and come with me." Nalivia shouted.

Anarigar reached for his scabbard and pulled out his sword. In the dim light, the bow and arrow were of no use. Nalivia's coal continued to light a path back towards the way they had just come.

The eyes glowed in the dark and watched their every movement forward. Inching closer and closer, Anarigar stepped beside Nalivia with his sword in hand, ready to strike.

Stopping, Nalivia held her hand outstretched as far as she could reach to light up the creature who was staring at them. No sounds of growls or hissing were heard, so Nalivia took a few smaller steps closer until the light fell upon the face that held the eyes.

"It is a skull!" Nalivia announced. Walking up to the skull, Nalivia saw the eyes were diamonds that caught the light and glittered in all directions sending prisms of color throughout the cavern.

Gasping, Nalivia declared, "Oh, that is so beautiful. I am sure the gems are meant to be a talisman for Boultori."

Reaching out to the skull to pluck one of the gems from the eye socket, Anarigar grabbed her hand quickly.

Anarigar hissed, "Don't touch them. The skull is a warning. This mountain is sacred, and that skull is protecting the spirits that rest here. You will be sorry if you take even one of them."

Nalivia shook her hand free of Anarigar's grasp. "My instincts tell me that the gems are important, and Boultori will need them. I must take at least one of them." Grasping one of the diamonds from the eerie skull's eye socket, Nalivia held it in her hand before Anarigar could try to stop her again.

Just then, the earth started to shake, and a rumbling was heard from where the two had entered. Anarigar turned to see small stones beginning to shift and tumble down from the mountain.

"We need to get out of here now before the opening is closed by the rock slide." Again, his warning cry was, "Run!"

Holding onto the gem, Nalivia ran as fast as her small legs would allow. The opening was already half-covered when they reached it, but Anarigar pushed Nalivia up and through the opening while scampering over the rocks and boulders covering the bottom half of the opening.

As they fell to the ground below, now outside of the cavern, more rocks cascaded down from the top of the mountain, covering the opening completely. The falling stones plummeted ever closer to where the two children lay. Anarigar used his feet to push himself back across the ground while pulling Nalivia with him. The rocks stopped just short of their feet.

"Whew! That was too close. I told you that something awful would happen if you took the gem. I think we should leave here quickly." Anarigar got to his feet and helped Nalivia do the same.

The ground started to shake once more and more violently. Looking up, Anarigar saw a huge boulder had broken loose from the top of the mountain was bouncing off the sides, heading towards them.

Grabbing Nalivia by the hand, Anarigar ran down the path back towards their camp with the boulder rolling in pursuit. Looking back, he saw the enormous rock was picking up speed. Bouncing from one side of the wall to the other, the boulder continued in the same direction the children ran.

Seeing the boulder was about to land on them, Anarigar pulled Nalivia backward and pushed her to the ground. Covering her body with his own, Anarigar was relieved when the boulder bounced over their bodies and landed tightly between the two walls blocking their return to the camp.

"Great!" Anarigar sarcastically said as he got to his feet and dusted off his clothes.

Looking down at Nalivia, he scowled. "We can't climb up those sheer walls. That boulder is too large to move or climb over for that matter. Look at the mess you got us into just because you would not listen to me when I told you not to touch the gem."

Nalivia got to her feet. In a pout, she said, "It is not my fault. I know I was supposed to take the diamond. We must think of a way to get out. Now stop blaming me and think."

"You are the sorceress. Do something. You have charms, use them to get us out of here," Anarigar rebutted.

Nalivia took stock of her charms. Most were untried. Using the trowel to dig under the boulder was a possibility, but she didn't know how long it might take. The hand trowel made quick work of the crack to enter the cavern, but would she be able to make a passable tunnel under the boulder?

There was little chance her piece of coal would make a fire intense enough to burn through solid rock. Nalivia had no idea how her crystalized teardrop would help since a rainstorm would only flood the area where they stood. Swimming out didn't seem like a good idea, either. Chances were that Anarigar could not swim anyway having lived in a desert all his life. That left the bumblebee's wing.

Representing air, Nalivia remembered Rowanda created a whirlwind that lifted her off the ground. Maybe her bumblebee's wing could do the same

Taking it into her hand, Nalivia thought of wind whirling, but nothing happened. She concentrated harder, and still, not a breath of wind blew within the walls.

"Well, I am waiting. You are a sorceress, aren't you?" Anarigar said mockingly.

Ignoring his jab, Nalivia decided to let her mind go blank. Anarigar's insults were no longer heard. Her eyes closed, and her mind emptied of thoughts. Feeling light as a feather, Nalivia felt as though she was floating in the air. A scream brought her out of the darkness, and she found herself hitting the ground hard.

"You were flying, Nalivia. You were really flying!" shouted Anarigar. "How did you do that?"

Nalivia rubbed her bruised knees as she got to her feet. "I was flying?"

"Yes, you were flying around in the sky. Can you do it again...and can you make me fly, too?" Anarigar asked in excitement.

Nalivia shook her head. "I have no idea what I can do. All I can do is try again. Hold onto my hand, and don't let go no matter what happens."

Anarigar grabbed hold of Nalivia's hand so tightly that she yipped. "Not that hard. You are hurting me."

Holding on tightly, but not so tight that Nalivia was in pain, Anarigar watched as Nalivia closed her eyes again. Time passed, but Anarigar remained silent.

"Close your eyes, too. I think you weigh me down with thoughts. I need you to let your mind go blank," Nalivia instructed.

Finding it difficult to let his mind go blank, Anarigar tried to do as he was told. Closing his eyes tightly, Anarigar thought of nothing in particular and everything at once. Slowly, his mind stopped racing, and his thoughts diminished.

Feeling weightlessness was a strange sensation, and he was tempted to open his eyes but resisted when Nalivia squeezed his hand as a reminder. A gentle breeze caught his garments, and his robe whipped around his legs. His sleeves fluttered against his wrists.

Not being able to resist, Anarigar opened his eyes. Below was the boulder that had blocked their escape. A considerable force pulled him and Nalivia down on top of the boulder. Landing hard, Anarigar continued to slip off the side of the colossal stone, pulling Nalivia with him. Screaming in panic, Anarigar saw the ground rushing towards his face rapidly and knew he was going to suffer severe injuries.

Just before hitting his face into the sand, the downward movement stopped short. Anarigar was within inches of the ground and frozen in space.

Nalivia hovered above Anarigar with his hand in her own. Opening her eyes, she drifted slowly to the ground, placing Anarigar on the hot sand, face down.

"You did it! You really got us over the boulder unharmed. I am sorry for all the mean things I ever said to you. You are amazing."

Anarigar continued to grovel until Nalivia blushed and told him to stop.

"You are embarrassing me. Stop it." Nalivia said, not meaning a word of what she was saying. She was enjoying Anarigar's praise.

Realizing he sounded like a fool, Anarigar stopped his prattle. "Do you think we can leave now? I would really like to go home."

Nalivia took inventory of the charms they had acquired while in the mountain. There was a bone, a blue gem, a petrified bat, and the diamond. That was only four charms, and Boultori would need more.

"I believe we need more charms for Boultori, so he has options. I feel we have gotten all the charms we are going to get from this source. Let's travel and see what might beckon me to a new source," Nalivia said.

Anarigar's eyes were rolling back into his head as he said, "You think? We are really going to look for another source? I want to go home."

Nalivia ignored Anarigar's sarcasm and told him, "I have a task to perform, and you are duty-bound to help. We will continue until I say we are finished!"

Breaking camp, the two mounted the drometarius and headed the direction back towards Anarigar's home. Nalivia didn't say a word as they traveled. Instead, she kept her mind quiet so she might feel any charm that was calling out to her.

Hours past. Nalivia was hot and tired from traveling in the heat of the day. Her mind was no longer at rest. Instead, she was feeling woozy and light-headed.

"I need to stop," Nalivia called out.

Anarigar dropped his drometarius to its knees and dismounted. Coming to Nalivia's aide, he helped her off the back of her drometarius. Sitting in the shade the animals provided, they each drank water and ate some food.

"You are just overheated. You will be fine. We will rest here until the heat of the day passes. Why don't you try to nap?" Anarigar said comfortingly.

Not responding, Nalivia let her eyes close and drifted off. Anarigar kept guard. He knew the drometarius would let him know if a terpor or wetchel approached, but other things in the desert could harm them besides animals.

He had just thought about approaching dangers when he saw a wall of sand looming that was so high there was no way Nalivia could make them fly above it. Alarmed, he shook the sleeping girl awake.

"We need to make a run for it. There is a sandstorm coming straight at us. Our only chance is to run for cover," Anarigar shouted in distress.

Throwing Nalivia onto the back of her drometarius, Anarigar jumped upon the back of his own mount. Rapidly getting to their feet, the two animals knew from instinct that they must run.

Galloping at full speed in the opposite direction of the fast-approaching sandstorm, the two animals moved at surprising speed. Nalivia held on with all her might and watched over her back to see if they would be able to outrun the storm.

Seeing the wall of sand gaining on them no matter how fast the drometarius were running, Nalivia grabbed her talisman and closed her eyes. She was not sure what to do next.

Stinging sand hit her in the back, and her drometarius let out a cry. Anarigar dropped his mount once again, and Nalivia's drometarius did the same.

The animals closed their eyes and nostrils to keep the sand out, and Anarigar pulled Nalivia to the other side of the animals so the drometarius' bodies would cushion the blasting sand. Nalivia kept her eyes closed, and her hand clasped tightly on all her charms.

"Make it stop," she whispered. "Make the sand stop."

Rain fell from the sky, knocking the sand down to the ground. The storm became a torrent and swirled around their feet in rivulets. The sandstorm was no longer a factor, but Anarigar panicked, feeling his footing slide out from under his feet as the water swept him away.

CHAPTER TWELVE

It was decided the evening before entering the palace gates that the nomads would assist Rowanda, Emeraza, and Beir by any means they could. The first step was to get all three safely into the palace city. From there, nomads would flood the streets to find out any gossip surrounding Boultori, while Rowanda and Emeraza remained hidden out of sight. Beirimor, too, would stay out of sight for the time being. He had only been gone for one month, and many city dwellers knew the king would be thrilled to have him in custody once more.

To alleviate suspicion, the nomads would set up stalls to sell their wares. The chieftain promised Emeraza not to sell any of the slaves he acquired during his time in the desert. That promise was difficult for the chieftain as he counted the lost pieces of gold in his head.

Emeraza spoke freely as they sat on cushions enjoying their evening meal the night before they were to enter the palace gates. "Once Boultori becomes king, and King Nashua is overthrown, there will be no need for slaves." That thought only made the chieftain sullener as he realized he would never get any reimbursement for the many slaves now in his possession.

"Give them a choice to join your caravan, and maybe you will have willing helpers. In the long run, these humans maybe even more profitable as part of your family. Many of them are craftsmen and can make lovely items to sell. If they choose to return to their own homes, you may not stop them. Rowanda has tasked the terpor to watch over them. I know you would not want hundreds of terpor to return to your camp if you repress the people under their protection, would you?" Emeraza said with a sweet smile on her face that somehow seemed to make the chieftain's heart sink.

The chieftain was beginning to realize that life as he knew it may not stay the same. He wanted to believe that things would be better for his people as well. He had no real choice but to align himself with these sorceresses. The mental picture of the terpors surrounding his camp made him feel weak inside.

The next morning, the nomad caravan was moving towards the gates to the palace city. Rowanda, Beir, and Emeraza rode in one of the litters carried by many stout men. The curtains were drawn against the harsh sun and wind. Rowanda and Emeraza wore veils to hide their faces as the city guards were known to check most litters. Before getting to the gates, Beir got out of the cart and took his place alongside the other men to help carry the litter through the gates. It was doubtful the guards would give him a second glance since he was acting like a slave.

The krerri walked alongside Rowanda's litter. As they stopped at the entrance of the palace city walls, guards huddled together to decide who would be the one to check the passengers held within. No one wanted to approach the krerri. Pushing the youngest guard-forward, it was determined he would be the one to take the risk.

"Contain those animals!" the guard commanded, trying hard to sound brave. "I need to see who is traveling inside the litter."

As the guard approached, the krerris' hair stood up at the base of their necks and along their spine, making them look even more substantial. Warning growls threatened the guard. Each krerri started to pace back and forth beside the litter, eyeing the young guard menacingly.

Stalling, the guard looked back at the other guards for support. Taking one step forward, the guard was halted by a voice as one head poked through the curtains of the litter.

Removing her veil, Emeraza said in a quiet voice. "Peace, young man. There is only a young girl riding in this litter and me. As you can see, I am elderly and cannot walk far, but if it would make you feel less threatened, I will climb out and walk through the gates."

Feeling foolish, and also afraid, the young guard took the initiative and told the old lady she could remain in the litter. The other guards at the gate did not debate his decision and waved the litter through, backing away from the krerris as they passed.

Rowanda was relieved they did not need to fight their way into the city or use magic. It was too early to give the king any warning of their approach. Finding Boultori was the first item on the agenda, but removing the king from power was just as important. However, Rowanda knew she needed her other two talismans to be able to help Emeraza with the power struggle that would ensue.

The chieftain directed his followers to the center of the palace city. Stalls were erected to sell goods. All must seem as standard as possible. The vendors knew guards would be by shortly to collect the taxes on their vending sites. Laws existed to raise money to enrich the king.

Another law that existed was no one was allowed to camp within the city walls. Anyone staying overnight must seek lodging. The payment for a room came along with a hefty tax that went directly to the king's coffers. Because of a significant amount of taxes, the nomads rarely stayed more than two days to do business in the city. In the past, the auction of slaves brought in enough money to cover the taxes while providing a healthy profit. Realizing now that Emeraza and Rowanda insisted the slaves be freed, the chieftain could only hope for the overthrow of the king. With his removal, the taxes would cease, and profitable trade would be possible.

Beirimor left to find rooms at the same lodging house as before when he, Rowanda, and Boultori came to rescue the mothers being held prisoners in the palace only a month ago. Beirimor surmised that Boultori might return to the lodge if he was not being held prisoner, but Beir knew it was a longshot.

Once out of the litter, Rowanda looked around. She saw trees surrounding the palace and knew if she were on higher grounds, she would be able to see gardens and flowers and the crops growing just outside the palace. She was happy to see how lush the area looked until she remembered that each tree, flowering plant, or mainstay crop took its toll on Neslora. Hoping that Nalivia and Anarigar would be successful in finding charms for Boultori was the only thing that kept Rowanda from feeling sad. She wanted both worlds to be lush and beautiful. She knew how hard it was to survive in the desert from just being there for a short time.

Emeraza followed Beirimor into the lodging house. A hot meal would be nice, she thought. "Beir, could we sit and have a meal before going up to our room? I think it might be advantageous to listen to gossip in the eating hall. I am also rather hungry."

Beir smiled at his mother. He had missed her all those years he was held a prisoner in the king's jail. "I wouldn't mind a hot meal myself. I will find a table. You and Rowanda wait here until I signal you to come."

Rowanda stayed by the side of her grandmother. She found it hard to believe that the Elder Sorceress was even her grandmother. Rowanda was intimidated by the older woman all her life, and now she was trying to get past the reserved exterior of her grandmother to know the woman within. The ride within the litter was silent, with only a few words spoken.

"Grandmother, this is where Beir, Boultori, and I stayed when we first got to the palace city to find Mother. It is not cozy or very comfortable, but I hope you will be able to rest before we need to face the king," Rowanda said respectfully.

Emeraza responded, "I will be just fine here. I know the bed won't be as soft as my own, but I expected hardships when I decided to come to Arolsen. What I did not expect was to see just how powerful you have become without any instruction. "

Rowanda beamed at her grandmother's praise. She was just about to say more when Beir waved for them to come to a table that was cleaned and prepared.

Beir assisted Emeraza to her seat. "The food isn't great, but it is plentiful. I will order food that I know won't upset our stomachs. There is no sense in becoming ill when we have so much to do." Beir said this with a wink, knowing how picky his mother was when it came to food.

Rowanda smiled behind Emeraza's back. The enter Neslorian village knew Emeraza was fussy about food. She grew her own vegetables and had fruit trees in her yard. She threw more away to the chickens than she ate since she would not eat any food that was bruised or overripe. This trip was going to be hard on Emeraza in more ways than one, especially with the inevitable showdown with the evil king.

That thought caused the smile to leave Rowanda's face. Thinking about King Nashua and Emeraza locked in a magical battle sickened Rowanda. Terrible things could happen to Emeraza and Neslora if King Nashua were as vile as he was said to be. Beir often told his wife during the evening how evil King Nashua could be when they thought Rowanda was asleep.

The whole world of Arolsen was barren, desolate, and enslaved due to the greed for money and power that the king exhibited. His cruelty was secretly known by all and rarely spoken amongst

114

themselves aloud for fear of spies. Rowanda's father was overheard to say one evening how King Nashua would turn a family member to spy upon their own family by the threat of torture, bribery or even using magical spells. This caused much distrust throughout the city.

Realizing that she and Nalivia would need to help in the battle made Rowanda very nervous. Her abilities were so unreliable. It seemed her powers were either too robust or too feeble. Practicing was out of the question. No one could know there were two sorceresses in the city. The king would find out and have time to formulate a plan. Catching the king unprepared might be the only chance they would have to put Boultori on the throne.

When the food was laid on the table, Rowanda found herself just picking at it. The thoughts and fears in her mind caused her appetite to diminish. Beir saw that his daughter was barely eating.

"Rowanda, even if you aren't hungry, try to eat most of your meal. We have plans to make and little time. This might be your only chance to eat for the rest of the day," Beir said.

Rowanda put another fork of food in her mouth and chewed. The fact that the food, now cold, had little flavor and did not serve as an incentive to eat more. She knew her father was correct, so she continued to bite and chew.

All three of them remained silent at the table. Beir and Emeraza strained to overhear the gossip. At one point, Beir told the women he was going to mingle a bit and see if he could learn more. They should remain at the table and continue to eavesdrop.

Many minutes later, Beir returned and said their rooms were ready. Rowanda and Emeraza would share one chamber, and Beir would sleep in the room next to them. Going up to the accommodations, Beir did not go straight to his room. Instead, he followed Emeraza and Rowanda into their room.

Emeraza snorted when she saw the barren-looking room. It had no flowers or any feminine touches. There were two beds with pillows thrown carelessly upon them and a small table with two chairs next to the window. Beir sat on one of the chairs. His conversation made Emeraza forget the room.

Beir looked out the window. It was still light outside and hot. His mind was whirling like a desert sandstorm. Taking his eyes off the road below, he turned and looked at Emeraza and said, "I learned that Boultori escaped while being forced to grow more plants. No one seems to know where he might be, but I overheard one group talking about how the king sent out guards in pursuit. Another group spoke about the king opening two confluences, sending forty guards to Neslora to abduct slaves. I also learned that the king is obsessed with recapturing Boultori and has delayed the return of the guards and slaves from Neslora."

"That is a good thing!" Emeraza volunteered. "We were prepared for guards entering Neslora, so the other sorceresses have a plan in place. Now we don't need to plan a breakout from prison to get Boultori free, and there will be fewer guards."

"Yes and no," continued Beir. "Yes, we don't need to break him out of jail, but he could be anywhere. Where should we look, first? We must get the chalice and seeds back for Rowanda or Neslora could become as barren as Arolsen."

Rowanda butted into the conversation between her father and grandmother, "I think Boultori would return to your oasis. King Nashua does not know where Boultori has been all these years, so why wouldn't Boultori return to someplace he feels is safe."

Beir looked at his daughter with even more awe and respect. "You are right. That is exactly what Boultori would do. I suppose that I could return and see if he is there."

"No," said Emeraza. "The nomads cannot stay in the palace city more than two days without the guards becoming suspicious. The chieftain said that they never stay for more than two days. I think we should ask the nomads to go to the oasis and bring back Boultori."

Beir shook his head. "But can we trust the chieftain to do that. He knows Boultori has the chalice and pouch of seeds. He knows how important they must be. Why wouldn't he just take Boultori to the king and sell Boultori and the charms to the king?"

Rowanda spoke up, "I will tell you why he won't betray us. There are over one hundred reasons why he will do as you ask." Rowanda winked at her father.

Beir laughed out loud. "You are correct. Of course, he would not want one hundred terpor circling his encampment again. I will go and talk with him in the morning. It would not be a good idea for the nomads to leave today anyway."

"They don't all need to travel to the oasis. That would take far too many days for everyone to go there," Emeraza complained. "I agree that they should leave after two days, but I feel the chieftain should send two of his fastest drometarius and men to ride them. They could reach Boultori quickly and have him return here. The rest of the nomads could leave after the morrow."

Rowanda was puzzled. "I thought we needed the nomads to help us overthrow the king. Why would we want them to leave in two days?"

Beir responded, "They would cause too much suspicion in the palace if they stay longer. A large number of people massed in the center of the palace city would be a threat to the king. It is better that they leave. Besides, our plan will work better if we are stealthy. We need to catch the king, unaware. We also need to lay low until Nalivia and Anarigar return with charms for Boultori. We will need all the magic we can muster to overthrow King Nashua if his wizard powers are as strong as I fear."

Rowanda could see the benefits of being sneaky. She did not relish the idea of being stranded in this small, gloomy room for days. "Can we explore the city while we are here. I don't think Emeraza will be able to stand to be in this small room for days."

Emeraza immediately caught on to the fact that Rowanda was using her as an excuse to be able to leave the room. She responded quickly to the child. "Don't be concerned about me, young child. I can stand most anything if it means securing Neslora's future."

Realizing that Emeraza was aware of her ruse, Rowanda tried another approach. "I think I should go with you to talk to the chieftain. If he sees me, he will remember the terpor, and you won't need to threaten him. I don't think we need to intentionally try to scare him into doing our bidding, do you?"

Rowanda smiled sweetly at her father and waited for him to see that she was correct. Emeraza was the one who came to her defense.

"I agree with Rowanda. It would be better to allow the chieftain to keep his respect. A small visual reminder of Rowanda's powers would be much kinder than a verbal threat. We would like him to remain an ally, but if we insult him, we will lose his friendship forever. It would be good if the nomads were friendly to Boultori when he replaces King Nashua."

Beirimor reluctantly agreed to take Rowanda to see the chieftain in the morning. Beir bid his mother and daughter a good night and left to sleep in his own room.

The morning light streamed into the room, falling harshly onto Rowanda's face. She turned her back to the window and tried to fall back to sleep. A knock at the door made that idea impossible.

Emeraza rose from her bed and went to the door. Beir was standing in the doorway with a tray of food.

"We aren't even allowed out of the room to eat?" Emeraza asked incredulously.

"Oh, I'm sorry. I thought I was doing you a favor so that you would not need to mingle with the rowdy crowd. The crowds have already started to gather in the hall," Beir said as he pushed past his mother to lay the tray on the small table.

Rowanda jumped from her bed to see what delights might be for breakfast and was cheered to see eggs as part of the meal. Her face darkened at the thought that the eggs might be lizard eggs.

Rowanda looked at her father and said, "These aren't lizard eggs, are they?"

Laughing, knowing how much Rowanda detested lizard eggs, Beir replied, "No, Rowanda, these are good old chicken eggs. Sit down and eat. If you are going with me, I want you ready in a short time."

Beir left the room, closing the door behind him, leaving his mother and daughter to eat their breakfast. Beir was already up early, scouting where the chieftain would be found first thing in the morning. He discovered the chieftain was at the most excellent lodging house in the city.

Returning to Rowanda as promised, Beir left his mother to her own devices and left with Rowanda. The city roads were already crowded. Most people chose to do their shopping earlier in the day before the sun made being outside unbearable. Beir held Rowanda's hand so that they would not be separated as they navigated the crowd.

Entering the square in the middle of the city, Rowanda was mesmerized by all the colors and aromas. Barkers' cries rang out, trying to lure people to their stalls to buy their goods. Rowanda saw booths with food, carpets, clothing, scimitars, and livestock. The blended smells caused her to reach up with her right hand to pinch her nose. Spices filled her nose as well as the dung from goats and drometarius.

Passing through the center of the city found the luxurious accommodations the chieftain occupied while in the palace city. Two nomad guards remained outside the door and moved respectfully aside when they saw Rowanda.

Knocking at the door, another guard from within opened the door and allowed Beir and his daughter to enter. The chieftain was eating dates and enjoying an early glass of wine. Rising from the table, he greeted his guests and invited them to join him.

Rowanda eagerly accepted the offer and sat down at the table. Beir gave her a scowl to remind her that this was not a social call.

"Oh, come on," the chieftain said to Beir. "Let the child enjoy some of the delicacies our world has to offer. I am sure your world does not have some of these tasty treats."

Beir relaxed and joined the chieftain at the table. Watching Rowanda eating dates and a strange mixture that Beir, himself, had never tried, he was amused at Rowanda's reaction.

"This is absolutely delicious," Rowanda said as she put more of the gooey paste onto a cracker. "Don't spoil it by telling me what it is. I want to be happily ignorant. If you told me it was lizard intestines or something else horrible, I would stop eating it, and I am enjoying it too much to stop."

The chieftain had grown quite fond of the little sorceress. Smiling affectionately, he said, "I promise that I won't tell you that it is the eyes of a drometarius."

Watching Rowanda scramble for anything in which to spit the contents of her mouth, the chieftain laughed harder. "I am just kidding. It isn't eyeballs."

Seeing Rowanda start to relax, the chieftain added, "It is something much worse."

Rowanda caught the gleam in his eyes and knew...or hoped he was just teasing her. Rowanda laughed as well and took one more cracker on which to spread the sticky goo.

The chieftain looked to Beir to explain the early morning interruption. "I am assuming this is not a social call."

Beir took his cue and answered. He explained about Boultori's escape and the idea that Boultori may have returned to the oasis. Beirimor asked whether the chieftain might send riders to fetch Boultori back to the city. Beir also told the chieftain that his nomads were released to continue their journey unless recalled by Rowanda.

The chieftain listened carefully and asked, "How will we know if we are to return to assist you in any matter if we are wandering the desert?"

Beir knew this was the moment he could remind the chieftain of his daughter's powers. "You will know when terpors encircle your encampment. No harm will come to any of the nomads, but it will be a sign that we need for you to return in haste."

All humor left the eyes of the chieftain at the mention of terpors surrounding his encampment. Quickly, he let Beirimor know he understood precisely what he was being told.

"We will leave by the end of the afternoon when the sun is starting to set. I would rather not start our travels in the heat of the day. Will that work with your timetable? I will send out two riders immediately to see if Boultori is at the oasis you mentioned."

The chieftain called his guard to his side and gave the order to send out two riders immediately as he promised. As the guard left the room, Beir said that they had interrupted the chieftain's morning way too long and indicated to Rowanda that she should excuse herself from the table.

Rowanda came to Beir's side, but before they left, the chieftain gathered treats to send with Rowanda, much to her delight. Rowanda was anxious to return to Emeraza to share the delicacies. Thanking the chieftain, he was pleased with the evident joy on the child's face. Beir did not miss the fact that the chieftain seemed genuinely smitten with the little sorceress.

With a respectful bow, the two left the room and made their way down the stairs and back into the streets. Once again, amongst the throng of people, Beir became protective of his daughter. He cleared a pathway through the multitude to allow her to pass unharmed. The jostling of the masses could injure a young girl who was unused to the crowding and pushing.

Halfway through the city center, Beir heard the loud purring as the krerris came to greet the young sorceress. Rubbing against her legs and demanding attention from the girl was not missed by most of the people passing widely around the spectacle. None of the city dwellers wanted to get within touching distance of the krerris but wondered at the sight of one small child commanding such attention from the large cats. Most could see the girl was not a nomad by her dress.

As the krerris' handlers came to retrieve the animals, they saw the child, Rowanda, and bowed respectfully. Again, the people of the city did not miss this fact.

Chatting for a short time with the handlers, Rowanda gave each krerri a dismissal pat on the head and followed Beir with a wistful glance back at the large cats. Thoughts filled Rowanda's mind.

"Father, when we get home, may I have a pet? I thought it might be nice to have a krerri of my own, or maybe a wetchel to ride. Would Grandmother allow me to take one home when we return?" Rowanda inquired.

"You will need to ask your grandmother, but I would not get my hopes up if I were you. You would probably receive a positive answer if you asked for a house cat, but not a krerri. You know your grandmother was frightened of them. She definitely will say no to a wetchel. You can count on that." Beir moved Rowanda down the smaller road that led back to their lodging, entirely unaware that they were being followed.

CHAPTER THIRTEEN

 Nalivia watched in horror as Anarigar was swept away by the torrent of water she had created. Thinking fast, Nalivia reached for her charms and grasped her hand trowel. Throwing it just in front of Anarigar, Nalivia commanded a plant to sprout hastily.

Screaming in pain, Nalivia saw the plant that Anarigar was clinging to was a cactus. Her plan to cause a plant to grow quickly did not take into account that a natural plant of this world would be the one most likely to sprout.

"I'm sorry! Anarigar. I didn't mean for a cactus to grow. I just thought any plant you could grab hold of would stop you from being swept away," Nalivia said, almost in tears.

"Ouch! That hurts," Anarigar complained as he pulled out cactus thorns. "Those spines really hurt, but I suppose I need to thank you from saving me from drowning—something you caused, by the way."

Nalivia was offended now. "I just saved your life, and now you are blaming me for causing the rain?"

"Come on. Let's just get out of here before you cause another disaster," Anarigar sniped.

Nalivia stomped off towards her drometarius and managed to get on its back without any assistance from Anarigar. Anarigar did the same, and soon the two were heading in the right direction.

After many minutes of not speaking, Nalivia shouted at Anarigar to stop. Spotting something unusual in the sand, the young apprentice wanted to investigate. Nalivia felt as if the item was calling to her.

Sliding off the drometarius' back, Nalivia walked cautiously toward the item. Nudging it with her foot, Nalivia discovered only a small part of the item was above ground.

"What is it?" asked Anarigar as he came up behind Nalivia to see what had caught her eye.

"I don't know for sure. I will need to uncover it to find out," Nalivia said as she got to all fours and started to move the sand from the object.

Uncovering it, she discovered the item was a forked piece of wood. It was sanded smooth from years of being in the desert.

Anarigar looked closer. "I think it is a petrified branch from an olive tree. I was told that there were groves of olive trees that once grew here before this all became desert."

Curious, Nalivia asked, "You mean this was not always arid land? I just assumed Arolsen has always been nothing but desert. If there were groves of olive trees once, it must have been totally different than it is today."

"Well, not in my lifetime. I have never known anything but a desert. My grandfather told me that his father talked about how many plants grew on his land when he was a boy. My great-grandfather said they had date trees, pomegranate, cocoa, coffee, and grains of all sorts. The way my grandfather talked, it was as if great-grandfather must have exaggerated quite a bit. But this olive tree branch didn't just blow here in a sandstorm. It has been here for many years. Besides, there are no olive trees anywhere, near or far, from here. Maybe my great-grandfather really did grow everything that he claimed."

Nalivia tucked the olive tree branch into her belt. "I think this could be a charm that would claim Boultori. It is worth taking to him to find out. That makes five talismans that may choose Boultori. We need to keep searching. I feel like time is becoming our enemy."

As evening approached, Anarigar announced, "We are almost back to my home. I don't think you are going to find any more charms. We will spend the night with my father and tomorrow, we will go to the palace city to find Beirimor and Rowanda."

Nalivia clapped her hands. "Oh, goodie. I have missed Rowanda. I will be happy to see her again and tell her about our adventures. I think Elder Emeraza will be impressed with the charms I have found. It never hurts to be in the good graces with the Elder Sorceress."

Anarigar admitted, "She scares me. Is she always so stern?"

"Oh, my, yes. I have never seen the Elder laugh," Nalivia confessed. "For years, we thought she was depressed because she lost her son, but even this past month, when Beirimor returned, I have not seen her smile. She cried when she saw Beirimor, but she did not smile. Odd, don't you think?"

"I don't know. People who hold high positions of power and authority have much on their shoulders. I suspect she is not depressed as much as weighed down by all the responsibility," Anarigar said, sounding very grown-up.

As they continued their journey home, Nalivia rode beside Anarigar. She told him the story her mother told her.

"Probably about the same time that your great-grandfather was alive, I was told that Neslora was not a very nice place to live.

Everyone toiled hard to make a living. Plants grew, but not well. It seems that some years there would be droughts, and some years there were pest infestations. My mother told me that around that time, the very first sorceress, named DuyVessa, discovered her powers. She discovered she had a connection with nature. After that, Neslora became a paradise. Plants grow by command, and even cut flowers bloom eternally with just a flick of the wand."

"That sounds too good to be true," Anarigar said in disbelief.

"Oh, it is true," Nalivia confided. "Neslora is beautiful and good. All the creatures live in harmony. It really is paradise. The only time we have had any trouble was when King Nashua caused a confluence to open, and soldiers came into our world and abducted our people. Well, I should also clarify that we have had trouble since Rowanda left the chalice and pouch of seeds behind to help your world."

At the return of the two drometarius, all the goats started bleating together. The racket caused so much noise that Anarigar's father rushed out to see if wetchels were surrounding the herd. Observing the return of his son, Anarigar's father ran to meet the two children.

"I am so glad to see you, my son. I was beginning to think you might have gotten lost in the desert. You are just in time for supper. Come in. I will have your younger brother take care of the drometarius. You both must be tired, hungry, and thirsty. Come in. Come in," Anarigar's father said while crushing his son to his chest.

Taking Nalivia by the arm, Anarigar ushered her into his father's tent. Anarigar was greeted by his four brothers. Each one gave Anarigar a bear hug and danced him around the tent.

Anarigar's father stopped the foolishness and asked everyone to sit for dinner. He served his sons and their guest, himself. Fresh goat cheese, dates, and some items Nalivia could not identify were served to her. She ate everything gratefully and offered to do the dishes.

"No child, you must be tired from your travels. Anarigar has told me of your plans to go to the palace city tomorrow morning. It is better if you retire early. My sons will take care of the dishes. We do all the cooking and cleaning since Anarigar's mother was abducted many years ago. We each have duties. I thank you for your kind offer, but I must insist that you rest."

Nalivia was shown where she was to sleep. Admittedly, she was exhausted.

Anarigar stayed up for several more hours telling his brothers and father of the adventures at the sacred mountain as well as the sandstorm and the torrential rains Nalivia caused.

"You mean that little girl commanded rain out of the sky in the desert?" Anarigar's father said in disbelief.

Anarigar shook his head, indicating an affirmation. "Yes, father. You can't believe what that little girl can do. We really flew!"

"No way!" shouted all of his brothers in unison. "You are just lying now," his older brother said in disbelief.

"No, really, we did. We were trapped behind a huge boulder and the walls of the canyon. There was no way to get out. She told me to empty my mind and close my eyes. The next thing I knew, we were flying over the boulder."

"No way!" was the chorus again.

Anarigar yawned. He excused himself to go to his sleeping quarters while his brothers chattered away like magpies.

In the morning, Anarigar's brothers had even more questions at breakfast. Nalivia smiled at the praise she received from Anarigar. She repeatedly blushed as he told the stories over and over, adding more details each time.

"It is getting hot, my son," Anarigar's father announced. "Your provisions are packed on the drometarius. Even though I do not want you to leave us again, I understand how important it is for Boultori to receive the charms you have found for him. If we are ever going to rid Arolsen of the evil king, you must go. Time is precious."

Thanking Anarigar's family for their hospitality, Nalivia took out her trowel and caused a small grouping of fig trees to sprout. In the time it took Nalivia to follow Anarigar to the waiting drometarius, the fig trees were already three meters tall.

Nalivia was proud that she was now able to mount without assistance. She felt quite comfortable on the animal and sensed it did not mind her riding on its back at all.

Waving goodbye, Anarigar took the lead, and Nalivia followed, looking back to see Anarigar's father and brothers dancing in glee around the new trees. Smiling, Nalivia thought how much she enjoyed magic when it made people happy.

The sun was low in the sky, but the heat was already intolerable. Covering as much of her body as possible to protect herself from the sun and to keep her body's moisture contained, Nalivia thought she was adapting quite well to the desert. She only hoped they would not encounter a wetchel as Rowanda was not there to make it into a pet.

Coming close to Beirimor and Boultori's oasis to refresh the drometarius with feed and water, smoke was noted rising from the main tent. Anarigar raised his hand for Nalivia to stop her drometarius.

"Someone has taken up residence in Beir and Boultori's tent. I think we should approach with caution. One never knows who might be waiting in the desert to steal what you have. Our supplies and drometarius would be quite valuable. Follow me, but don't dismount. Be ready to flee back to my father if I yell," commanded Anarigar.

"But I want to help you. You know that I have some powers. If there is someone who intends to hurt you, I am not going to leave you and flee!" Nalivia said in a harsh whisper.

"Come on, then, but be prepared for anything," Anarigar whispered back.

Getting off their mounts, the two approached the tent on tip-toes. Drawing his sword, Anarigar took the lead. Nalivia was uncertain which of her charms would be the best defense as she followed closely behind Anarigar.

Stopping at the flap to the main tent, Anarigar turned and put his finger to his lips indicating Nalivia should be extra quiet. Lifting the flap, Anarigar saw no one inside.

"Aha!" came a booming voice from behind them.

Startled beyond the control of their fear, Anarigar dropped his sword while Nalivia screamed. Visible goosebumps popping out all over her legs and arms and not from being cold.

"Boultori! You gave me the scare of my life. What are you doing here?" Anarigar shouted in a high-pitched voice.

"And where did you find this little lizard, Anarigar?" said Boultori as he sized up Nalivia.

"This little lizard is here to give you magic charms that you can use against your brother," said Nalivia in disgust. "And, you must give me Rowanda's charms to give back to her."

"Whoa! Stop. I think we should all go inside the tent so that you can tell me what you are talking about," said Boultori, holding the flap of the tent open.

Once inside, sitting with a refreshing drink, the two children told Boultori what was happening. After much competing chatter between Anarigar and Nalivia, Boultori seemed to understand the dynamics of the situation.

"Little Lizard, I just returned from Neslora. Salitha, one of your sorceresses, inform me of how the use of the chalice and pouch of seeds here in Arolsen has caused destruction to Neslora. I learned that Rowanda has come back to retrieve them," said Boultori in clarification. "I also learned Beir, Rowanda, and the Elder Sorceress is in the palace city to rescue me, so we can overthrow my brother."

"That is right, except I arrived with them and was tasked to find talisman for your use," Nalivia said. "We must all hurry to the palace city. The sooner we get the chalice and pouch back to Rowanda, the sooner your brother will be dethroned."

"Twice, you said you have charms for me. What do you mean?" asked Boultori of Nalivia.

Nalivia laid all the items she and Anarigar had collected on the floor at Boultori's feet. "I am afraid that I do not know the spell to allow the charms to choose you, but Emeraza knows it. If we take all these charms to Emeraza, she will instruct you as to how to allow the charms to make themselves known to you. I can only show you what she did when my charms picked me."

"Go ahead. Show me what the sorceress had you do. It will not hurt for us to try. I think it would be to our advantage for me to have charms before entering the palace city. I am not unknown there and entering will be tricky. If charms might help me to enter, then it is worth a try. Show me, okay?" Boultori instructed.

Nalivia laid all the charms on the small table, spreading them out. "Usually, you would have twice as many charms from which to choose. I mean, there would be more charms to select you since they pick you and not the other way around. Let's just hope four out the five want to belong to you." Under her breath, Nalivia said, "but I can't imagine why any of them would want to choose an ill-mannered man like you," still feeling offended by being called little lizard.

"Now, I want you to close your eyes, and let your hands, palms down, spread out across the table. Slowly move them back and forth, but don't open your eyes. If you feel nothing at first, allow your hands to drop closer to the table. If you feel any sensations at all, let me know. You might feel a prickling, burning, cold sensation, or something unusual. Don't touch anything until I say you can. Are you ready to try?" Nalivia said sounding less than confident.

Anarigar watched as Boultori did as instructed. Closing his eyes and allowing his hands to float freely above the table, he let his mind relax and just feel.

"Do you sense anything at all?" Nalivia asked impatiently.

"Yes, actually, I do. My stomach is growling, and my feet are itching." Boultori said in his usual jest.

"That does it. We will gather the charms and wait for Emeraza to conduct the spell. You won't act like such a fool when she is around," Nalivia growled. Just as Nalivia was about to gather the items, Boultori told her to stop.

"Wait! I do feel something. My fingers are tingling. In fact, I feel the heat emanating just below my right hand," Boultori said in astonishment.

Nalivia looked to see which items were right below Boultori's right hand and identified the diamond. "Keep your eyes closed, reach down gently and give it to me," Nalivia said with excitement in her voice. She never thought the spell would work without Emeraza, but it became clear a sorceress was not needed for charms to pick a wizard.

"Go on and see if any of the other items pick you," Nalivia urged.

Boultori allowed his hands to move slowly over the table. Feeling nothing, he listened as Nalivia told him to slowly lower both hands and continue the search.

Vibrating on the table, the olive branch seemed to be alive as it jiggled up and down. "I think you have found your next charm, Boultori. It is almost dancing for you. Reach down and take it. Place it in my hand."

Anarigar stood transfixed as the second, third, and finally, the fourth charm made themselves known to Boultori. Once all four charms were in Nalivia's hands, she told Boultori to open his eyes.

Looking at the odd assortment of items in Nalivia's hands, Boultori asked her if she knew what each might represent.

Handing Boultori the diamond, Nalivia told him she thought it represented Fire since he felt heat and tingling when his hand was over it, especially since the diamond is made from compressed coal. She went on to explain what she believed the other three items might be.

"The forked olive branch is a dowsing rod. If I am correct, it will represent the element Water. The petrified bat would represent Air, I am sure. The bone would be Earth since all bones return to the Earth eventually. Of course, I could be totally wrong. You will know more when we talk with Emeraza or when you try to use them."

Noting the one charm lying on the table, Nalivia picked it up and held it out to Anarigar. "This beautiful blue gem belongs to you, Anarigar. Wear it around your neck as a talisman. I know it will protect you and your family."

Anarigar cautiously took the blue gem between his fingers and held it up to the light. It sparkled and warmed to his touch. Never believing that he had an ounce of magic in his soul before this moment, he found himself connected with the stone.

"I can feel the stone. It is warming in my hand. Does that mean anything?" Anarigar asked, not taking his eyes off the blue gem.

Boultori answered, "If it means you have an ounce of magic ability within you, I will be offering you a position at the palace. You don't want to be a shepherd for the rest of your life, do you?"

"I have three brothers. I don't think my father would miss me much. I would love to explore any possibility that I might have the ability to become a wizard someday." Feeling almost giddy, Anarigar fingered his new gem and held it close to his heart. "I will need a pouch to carry my gem close to my heart at all times."

Boultori looked around his tent. "I know I made a pouch out of goatskin last year. It is the softest skin. I worked it night after night for a good moon. Oh, here it is. Just attach that sinew, and you will be all set."

Handing the pouch to Anarigar, Boultori ransacked the tent looking for his own bag. It was larger and had intricate designs stamped on it. Other than the dowsing rod, all of Boultori's charms fit nicely into the pouch. Like the rest, Boultori chose to wear it around his neck, letting the pouch rest near his heart.

"We still have daylight left to ride. Can you two share a drometarius so I can ride the other one?" Boultori asked as he went to the tent, gathering supplies and extra clothing.

"I guess we can double up. However, Nalivia, I don't want you chattering away in my ear the whole time," Anarigar sniped.

Nalivia didn't answer. She was too angry to even speak. Instead, she plotted her revenge. She would get even with Anarigar for his insult, even if she only hummed the same annoying song for the entire ride to the city. She let the most annoying songs go through her head until she found the one that she would hum. A smile formed on her lips as she picked the exact song.

"You are in trouble now, Anarigar!" Boultori said when he saw the smile cross Nalivia's face and noted the devilish gleam in her eye. "You never should insult a sorceress. You are more of a fool than I have ever been."

"What... What did I do?" whined Anarigar, acting innocent.

Grabbing his satchel, Boultori added snickering, "You'd better hope your new blue gem really has protective powers."

Nothing more was said. Anarigar just hoped Nalivia would forget the insult and settle into the rhythm of the drometarius' sway and go to sleep. Moving across the sand, Nalivia started to hum a little ditty from her world. At first, Anarigar didn't mind since it seemed to calm the girl. After an hour of the same sounds coming from her lips, over and over, Anarigar was about to scream.

Turning his body to confront the girl, Anarigar said, "Okay, you can stop. I get your point. You are mad at me for telling you not to chatter in my ear. That was rude of me. I am sorry, so stop."

Nalivia was about to hum even louder when she noticed several tunnels of sand moving in their direction. Her eyes widened as she grasped what that meant.

Seeing the look of horror on Nalivia's face, Anarigar turned forward to gaze in the same direction. Immediately, he whipped his drometarius into a full run, leaving Boultori stunned momentarily. Gathering his wits, Boultori, too, sent his mount in pursuit of the other drometarius.

"They are gaining on us," shouted Boultori. Noting the tunneling serpents were spreading out, Boultori understood they would be surrounding the trio in a matter of moments.

"Stop and dismount!" cried Boultori.

Anarigar, too, had assessed that there was no place to go. Listening to Boultori's command, Anarigar stopped his drometarius, and the two children scrambled off.

Both of the males grabbed their swords, and Nalivia's hand found her pouch grasping for a charm that may be used as a weapon against the three serpents who now confronted them.

Raising to their full heights and swaying menacingly back and forth, the three serpents slowly moved closer to their intended victims. The drometarius balled in fear but remained crouched on the sand, knowing they could not outrun the terpors.

Boultori took a defensive stance and faced one of the terpors, while Anarigar faced the second. Nalivia noting one terpor slithering up closer to her, turned to face it down, hoping she would grab the correct charm when the serpent went to strike.

Instead, the colossal snake lowered itself to the ground and slithered around to the other two serpents, blocking the land between the travelers and the path they intended to go. All three terpors turned their bodies and slowly moved in the direction the travelers needed to go.

"Is that odd or what?" Boultori asked in astonishment. "Why didn't they attack, and why are they now going the same way we need to go? Should we detour and go to the city from a slightly different angle?"

Nalivia was the first to answer Boultori. "No, I think they are going to lead the way for us. If we change directions, I believe they will, too. Look! They have stopped, and they are waiting for us."

Anarigar said with fear in his voice, "I don't like this. This is not the way terpor are supposed to act. We should be dead right now, and instead, you are saying we should follow them?"

Boultori rose and went to his drometarius. "Let's mount up and follow...but at a discreet distance."

Once back into a slower rhythm of riding the drometarius, the three stayed on alert. Expecting the terpor to reverse and return to strike at any moment, the ride became anything but relaxing.

Ever watching the three terpor in the lead, Boultori was amazed to see the serpents duck back into the sand and tunnel away as quickly as they came. To his surprise, a cloud of dust announced the advancement of two riders, and Boultori decided the terpor did not like the new odds and that is why they left.

Stopping his mount, Boultori allowed Anarigar and Nalivia to ride to his side. "Now what? I am sure we were a sight to see with three serpents leading two drometarius."

"Nomads," answered Anarigar, "but there are only two of them. I don't think we need to fear them. It is not likely they will rob us when we outnumber them. Be on the alert, though, just in case."

"Hail, Boultori," shouted the rider in the lead.

"Hail," returned Boultori as a greeting.

"You have saved us many hours in the hot sun searching for you. We are delighted to see you this close to the palace city. We will accompany you to the rest of the way. Beirimor and Rowanda await your arrival," the nomad in the lead announced.

As the company rode back into the searing sun, Boultori made casual conversation. "Did you, by chance, see the terpor that were traveling just in front of us?"

"Oh, yes, we did," was the casual reply. "I am sure Rowanda sent them to guard you until we could find you."

"Rowanda sent terpor to guard me? That is just preposterous. You have been out in the hot sun too long, and it has muddled your brain." Boultori could not comprehend such an idea.

"No, really. Rowanda has the power to charm the terpor. They are all under her control. Hundreds of them surrounded our encampment when we first captured Rowanda, Beirimor and the Elder Sorceress. We are now allies, and we intend to help overthrow your brother and put you on the throne. I hope you will remember us when you come into power," the second nomad said humbly.

Boultori did not respond. He was too busy trying to sort everything out in his mind. It was crazy-talk. Boultori knew Rowanda was a sorceress but controlling the terpor was nuts. No one could control the terpor. Boultori was about to say such when the second nomad continued his story.

"Rowanda has completely charmed our krerri as well. They act like house cats whenever they see her. They purr and rub up against her legs—well, body since she is small, and they are so large. They would protect her with their dying breath. Not only that, Beirimor told us how Rowanda charmed a wetchel, and they rode one as if it was a drometarius. I would have liked to have seen that."

Boultori broke into laughter. "I would have loved to have seen Beirimor on the back of a wetchel. I can't wait to rib him about that. You are telling me the truth when you say Rowanda has powers over the wild creatures of our world."

The two nomads just nodded their heads enthusiastically to show the answer was a big yes. They rode on in silence, watching the sun start its descent.

"With luck, we will just make it to the gates before they close the doors for the night. We should go faster just to make sure we arrive on time," one nomad said as he pressed his drometarius into a trot.

The quicker pace helped to assure their arrival just as the guards were rushing the last people into the walls. In their haste to close the doors, the guards neglected to check the last arrivals, and Boultori was relieved to enter unnoticed by the guards.

CHAPTER FOURTEEN

 Rowanda and Emeraza had plenty of time to get to know each other while being confined to the small room, or that is what they thought. After returning home from seeing the chieftain, Rowanda and Emeraza were sitting at the table, enjoying a snack that Beirimor had personally delivered. He told them to stay put, and he would be back shortly.

Rowanda complained that she wanted to go along with Beir as he scouted the city, but an emphatic no to her request stopped Rowanda in her tracks. After her father left, Rowanda asked Emeraza some questions, hoping her grandmother would be open to the conversation.

"Grandmother, when did you know that you were a sorceress? How did your mother prepare you if she was not a sorceress herself? How is it that you became the Elder Sorceress?" Rowanda didn't even give her grandmother a chance to answer the first question before she fired the next two.

Emeraza held up her hand to stop Rowanda's questions. She chewed the food that was in her mouth before she attempted to answer the first question.

"Well, that was all a very long time ago. I will need to think for a moment before I can answer your question," Grandmother Emeraza replied.

Rowanda thought that the time it took Emeraza to chew her food should have been plenty of time to gather her thoughts. At least, it seemed to Rowanda that the older lady chewed for an unnecessarily long time for the small amount of food that she had placed in her mouth.

"Let me see," Emeraza said, stalling a bit longer. "I guess I will start with the question as to how my mother prepared me when she was not a sorceress herself. Actually, she did not prepare me. Never being a sorceress, she was not aware of the small changes I was exhibiting. It was my grandmother who first noticed that I was starting to show signs of being a sorceress."

"What were the signs, Grandmother? I was not aware of any signs that I was a sorceress. I was just wondering if I had some signs that I missed as well. If I knew what your early changes might have been, I might be able to recall if I was aware of my own."

Emeraza stared at the wall as she concentrated. "The first thing my grandmother noticed was my ability to keep flowering plants in bloom for long periods of time. It seems my mother loved flowers, but she had no success with plants. Because I knew my mother loved flowers so much, I paid a lot of attention to the flowers in our garden. I talked to the plants and caressed the blooms. I remember taking joy in my mother's gardens, not so much because I liked flowers, but because she loved them."

Rowanda said, "I never spent much time in the garden, Grandmother Salitha was the one who tended our gardens, so I guess I didn't exhibit that specific gift. How is it that you knew I could be a sorceress?"

Emeraza was about to answer that question when there was a knock at the door. Rowanda started to go to the door but was halted by her grandmother.

"I will answer the door, Rowanda. You sit down and finish your snack."

Opening the door, Emeraza saw four guards standing in the opening. One of them stepped inside the threshold, making it impossible for Emeraza to close the door.

"Grab your cloaks. You will come with us to the palace. The king would like to make your acquaintance," the guard said with no emotion in his voice.

"But we were just eating. Couldn't we come to the palace later after we have finished?" Emeraza said politely, hoping to put off the guards.

"You will come now. The king has food at the palace. If you are hungry, I am sure the cook will prepare you a meal. We will leave now." The guards stepped through the door, making a barricade in case either the woman or child tried to make an escape.

Rowanda was about to say that they needed to wait for her father but decided it was best if Beir remained free. Somehow, Rowanda knew this would not bode well for them.

Slipping on their cloaks, Rowanda made sure her sword was covered entirely before the guards noticed she had a weapon in her belt. Emeraza covered her clothing with a cloak as well. Soon the four guards were marching Rowanda and Emeraza down the stairs and through the dining hall with all eyes glued to them. Stepping out into the blazing sun, Emeraza drew her cloak up over her head to protect her eyes. She reached down and took Rowanda's hand to give the child some comfort.

With two guards before them and two guards behind them, they were rushed through the city streets. Many eyes followed their progress, but each person quickly diverted their eyes when a guard would look their way. It was better not to see what was happening in the city if it involved King Nashua's guards.

Reaching the entrance to the palace, guards opened the gates and allowed the group to pass through, shutting the gates quickly behind them. Rowanda squeezed her grandmother's hand as much for Emeraza's assurance as to her own. They were about to meet the most powerful wizard in Arolsen, and that could not be good news.

The hallway leading to the throne room was as wide as several rooms in a typical house. The floors were polished to a shine, and Rowanda saw her own reflection as she glanced down at her feet. Looking up, Rowanda saw the ceiling was covered with small stones and gems, creating beautiful pictures of flying birds, fruit trees, and flowering vines. It reminded Rowanda of Neslora.

Suddenly coming to a halt, the guards waited for a command to enter. Standing in the same position for over an hour, a voice was finally heard to say 'ENTER.'

The guards from behind pushed Emeraza to make her move again. It almost seemed Emeraza had fallen asleep on her feet. Rowanda knew that was not the case. Emeraza was just trying to give the appearance of being a forgetful old woman. It would not do for anyone to know she was a sorceress.

Acting feebler by the moment, Emeraza leaned on Rowanda to reinforce the presentation of being frail. By the time they were standing in front of the king, Emeraza was swaying on her feet.

"Give the old woman a chair before she collapses!" shouted King Nashua.

Seeing the king for the first time, Rowanda did not see any resemblance to Boultori. King Nashua was tall, lean, and noticeably better looking than his short, silly-acting brother. However, King Nashua lacked any humor in his dark eyes. His smile was cruel, and his lips were kept tight, almost in a grimace. Whereas Boultori broke into a grin often and his eyes merrily sparkled with mirth.

Rowanda remembered thinking that Boultori could not be trusted when she first encountered him. Now that she was looking into the eyes of a devil, Rowanda knew what distrust looked like. Those were the eyes of evil.

King Nashua looked at Rowanda. Without letting his gaze leave her, he said, "Bring the child before me."

One of the guards grabbed Rowanda by the arm tightly and pulled her forward. "Ouch!" Rowanda involuntarily whined.

"I didn't say to hurt the child! I said to bring her before me. Can you do that without causing her pain? If not, maybe I should show you what pain feels like so you will be more compassionate in the future," King Nashua growled.

The guard immediately dropped to his knees, clutching his chest in agony. Rowanda stood helpless as the guard fell face-down on the shiny floor with blood escaping from his mouth.

"Get him out of here and clean up that mess immediately!" roared the king.

People rushed from out of nowhere to drag the guard from the room while others mopped the floor as quickly as possible. Never allowing their eyes to fall upon the king, the room was restored to order in a blink of an eye. Now, only three guards stood before the king.

"As I was saying, bring the child before me," reiterated King Nashua.

One of the guards gently laid a hand on Rowanda's back and guided her towards the throne. Stepping back into place, the guard's eyes focused on the wall behind the king, waiting for the next command.

The king turned his full attention to Rowanda. "So, child, I hear you have the ability to turn savage krerri into sweet little pussycats. I could use your talent with my own hunting krerri. I am offering you a position in my palace. What do you say to my kind offer?"

Rowanda looked towards Emeraza for some sign as to what to say or do, but Emeraza sat on the chair looking down at her folded hands. Rowanda realized Emeraza did not want to give away any signs of her having magical powers. Rowanda knew she would need to think this through herself.

"Your Highness, I only can charm those specific krerri because I helped to raise them from cubs," Rowanda lied.

"I see, so if I have my guards pursue the nomads that left this morning and capture the krerri you raised, you will be able to work for me, is that correct?" the king asked pointedly.

"Yes, Your Highness, that is correct. I would be able to control those krerri," Rowanda replied.

"I think you could control my krerri as well. I think you are just modest." King Nashua said darkly. "We will put it to the test. Have my krerri brought into the courtyard? Oh, also place the elderly woman there, too."

Rowanda knew she was being tricked. She would need to reveal her abilities, or her grandmother would need to expose her own powers. Rowanda knew it was essential to keep Emeraza's secret safe. That meant she would be required to calm the krerri and show herself to be a liar. Rowanda remembered what happened to the guard just moments before when he displeased the king. Rowanda wondered what her fate would be when the king saw she lied.

Emeraza was assisted from the sitting position and taken out of the throne room. The king got to his feet.

"Shall we follow the old woman to the courtyard?" King Nashua asked with false kindness in his voice.

Rowanda's mind raced. She thought about every charm she had on her body and wondered whether she could combine their forces to open a confluence and escape with Emeraza. That, however, would leave her father and Nalivia stuck in Arolsen. There must be a better plan. Rowanda chastised and thought to herself, 'think, think, think.'

Moving from one corridor after another corridor, Rowanda soon became confused as to which direction the throne room was. It would be easy to get lost in such a vast palace. Rebuking herself for not paying closer attention to the layout of the palace for future escape, Rowanda made a note of any detail from that point on. She hoped Emeraza had the presence of mind to be doing the same.

Soon, two guards and Emeraza departed down a different corridor while the king and the other guard ushered Rowanda into a large, luxurious bedroom with a balcony on the west side of the room. The guard guided Rowanda out onto the balcony, where she could look down into the courtyard below. Four krerri were prowling around the courtyard walls looking for a means of escape.

Rowanda watched as the krerri suddenly halted, and all their eyes turned towards the door to the palace that was opening. Emeraza made her appearance, and Rowanda could see the krerri becoming agitated. Fanning out, the four animals soon were surrounding Rowanda's grandmother.

Emeraza stood perfectly still with her eyes closed. Rowanda could sense her grandmother's presence in her mind. Directing Rowanda to quietly take her tiger's eye into her hand, Rowanda did as her grandmother mentally directed her to do.

As the one krerri behind Emeraza prepared its body to spring upon the old lady, the other three krerri pressed closer and closer, also getting ready to tear the old woman to pieces. Rowanda's eyes widened as she realized she must act immediately.

With one giant mental command, Rowanda halted the krerri in place. Not a single one moved a muscle. They seemed frozen in time.

King Nashua applauded. "I knew you were lying to me. Now, go down and meet your new charges. From here on out, you will stay with the krerri day and night. You will be at my beck and call, and when I tell you to be ready for a hunt, you and the krerri will be ready. Do you understand? Otherwise, I can find another way for the old woman to be torn into pieces."

"What will become of my grandmother? Can she stay with me? I have never been alone, and I am afraid." Rowanda didn't need to try hard to pretend she was just a scared little girl as she said this to the king.

"For now, your grandmother can stay with you. Displease me in any way, and your grandmother will be taken away, and you will never see her whole again."

King Nashua gave an order to the guards to take the child down to the courtyard to join her grandmother and her new charges. "Make sure they have a room right next to the krerris' kennels. I want the girl to be in constant contact with the animals. She is not to be allowed to run around the palace. That goes for the old lady as well. I want the krerri ready for a hunt tomorrow."

Rowanda was shown the way through the corridor and down the stairs to the courtyard. As she entered, the spell placed on the krerri was broken, and they raced to meet Rowanda. Acting just as the nomads' krerri reacted to her, Rowanda was greeted by purrs and rubbing against her body. Emeraza was allowed to move, but slowly.

Emeraza embraced Rowanda when she thought it was safe to do so. "Thank you, Rowanda, for saving my life. I didn't cherish the idea of being lunch for those krerri. I suspect they do not feed them sufficiently, so I was looking like fresh meat to them and nothing else."

A guard stood warily in the doorway. "When you are ready, I will show you to your room." It is evident that the guard knew to be deferential to the girl when the krerri were surrounding her. The guard had no doubt the animals would look at him as a threat if his voice sounded the least bit harsh.

"We will follow you now. I believe my grandmother would like to sit down. She is rather feeble, as you can see." Winking an eye unseen by the guard, Rowanda allowed a smile to form knowing the truth that Emeraza was anything but feeble

.

CHAPTER FIFTEEN

 Beirimor returned to the room to find Rowanda and Emeraza gone. He noted their cloaks were missing and feared they went out to the city to explore. Racing down the stairs, he stopped and asked the innkeeper if he saw them leave.

"I would be smart to keep my mouth shut. It does not pay to see anything that involves the king's guards if one wants to stay healthy, but since it was your mother and your daughter that was taken, I will tell you that much," the innkeeper said in a hushed voice.

Beir stormed out of the inn and bumped unceremoniously into three dusty hooded desert rats who were just entering the inn.

"Beir!" shouted Boultori as he grabbed his friend into a bear hug. "Where are you going in such a hurry?"

Beir stepped back in surprise. "I didn't expect you this soon. Quick, we must hurry." Realizing he had not even greeted his friend after not seeing him for a month, Beir added, "It is good to see you again, my old friend."

"I'm younger than you are, so who are you calling old?" joked Boultori, not sensing the dire mood Beirimor was exhibiting.

"No time for foolishness, Boultori. Your brother has Rowanda and my mother. We must go to the palace and free them NOW!" Beir said with panic in his voice.

"Wait! We can't just go storming into the palace. You do remember how many guards are under my brother's control. We need to find a safe place to make a plan. By the way, this is my new apprentice, Anarigar."

Beir seized Anarigar in an embrace, "It is good to see you again as well, Anarigar. And Nalivia, I didn't mean to slight you either. Once we find a quiet place to talk, you will need to tell me all about your adventures, but right now, we must make haste."

The two nomads were signaled to join the group to make plans, and they followed, watching behind their backs for anyone who may be tracking them. One of the nomads stepped forth and declared he knew the exact place they could all meet securely.

"Our chieftain has many friends in the palace city. Follow me, and I will take you to a room where we will be guarded. Many citizens despise the king and will help us to overthrow him."

Quickly following the first nomad, while the second one stayed in the rear to watch for anyone who may be following, the group moved through the streets to a side alley. Knocking on a door, a woman answered and stepped aside, recognizing the nomad as a friend.

"Can we use a room to make plans? We are about to revolt against the king!" the nomad announced but under his breath.

Showing the way to the largest room in the small house, the woman announced that her children would all stand guard. "I will place one of my children on the rooftop, and the rest will pretend to play outside, scattering to watch if anyone should approach."

Beir, suddenly curious, asked the nomad who the woman and children were. Answering, he said, "this is my family. I don't want them traveling the desert, so I keep this home for them. I am in the city often enough to provide for their every need. This way, they stay safe, and I have a home to visit when I am in the city."

Beir just shook his head. "If the living arrangement works for you, I am pleased. Please tell your wife and children how much we appreciate their hospitality and their assistance."

As the group sat upon cushions in the room, the nomad's wife came in with a tray filled with dates, goat cheese, and bread, and a pitcher of fresh water. One of the smallest children followed, carrying a tray of cups. Once she set it down, the little girl ran to her father, smothering him with kisses. With a pat on her head, he dismissed his child and smiled appreciatively at his wife as she too left the room.

Beir started the conversation, "I really want to hear everything that has happened to all of you, but I fear the stories must wait. We need to get a plan in place."

Looking at the second nomad, Beir asked if he would be able to ride out into the desert and locate his tribe. "We will need them to return as quickly as possible to help in the revolution. The guards at the gate, as well as the ones stationed in the city, must be dealt with if we are going to succeed."

With a quick explanation of his plan, the nomad got to his feet and exited the house. He knew his drometarius would balk at the thought of another long gallop in the broiling sun, but the animal would do as directed, especially since it was drinking its fill of water at the well.

Beirimor asked questions of Boultori, Nalivia, and Anarigar. "Were you successful in finding charms that bonded to Boultori?"

Nalivia and Anarigar told their tale as briefly as possible, leaving out all the exciting adventures. They knew Beir was interested in the facts only at this critical time.

Boultori opened his pouch and revealed his charms and also took the dowsing rod from his belt. "Once I can figure out how to use my talisman, I will be able to help with the take-down of my brother. I just wish Emeraza was here to guide me through the initial use of my new charms. Nalivia has explained which element each charm represents, but I have no idea how their use will play out. I may cause more destruction to us than to my brother." Boultori said without a hint of humor.

Beir knew Boultori was apprehensive about using his new charms. He also knew that Boultori witnessed firsthand how unreliable a charm could be in the hands of a sorceress with little experience controlling them. Reliving Rowanda whirling in the dust devil she had created herself, went through Beir's mind. Hoping nothing quite so comical happened when Boultori used his charms for the first time came as a serious thought. There was no room for mishaps.

"I am afraid the first time you use your charms will need to be at the palace gates. Nalivia will use her talisman as well, so be comforted that you won't be required to fight the guards by yourself. You mentioned Anarigar will be your apprentice. Does that mean he also has some potential?" Beir asked, trying to assess the abilities of his companions when the fight would start.

Nalivia spoke up first, "Anarigar has a blue gem that should protect him. We don't know whether he can control the gem. Why we didn't make an effort to have Anarigar test it in the desert is beyond me. We were in a rush to get Boultori here with Rowanda's chalice and the pouch of seeds."

"That's right. I almost forgot the main reason we returned to Arolsen. Nalivia, I want you to take the chalice and pouch and keep them safe. King Nashua will most likely overlook you when the fighting begins. Boultori, however, will be the main focus of the king. He will want to destroy his brother to make sure Boultori cannot take his throne."

"I didn't need to hear that right now," Boultori said with some misgivings. "My brother is as mean as a terpor. I know he will not want me alive if I cannot benefit him. Maybe I should hang on to the chalice and pouch just to give Nashua some reason to keep me alive."

Beir responded, "The chalice and pouch will not keep you alive now. Your brother will be aware we are at his gates to kick him out of power. The thought that he could use you to make Arolsen lush and green will mean nothing if he loses power. No, he will definitely try to kill you."

Nalivia spoke up, directing her statement to Boultori, "I didn't like you much when you called me a little lizard, but I have grown fond of you. I won't let your brother kill you."

"Great. That makes me feel really safe." Boultori said sarcastically and immediately amended what he said when he realized how awful his words sounded to the child who wanted to protect him. "I really mean that, Nalivia. I do feel safer knowing you have my back. I didn't mean for it to sound so sarcastic."

Nalivia was soothed. She had bristled at his words when Boultori spoke them out of fear, but Nalivia found she could understand Boultori much better after spending time with him. She knew him to be a kind man who always wanted to appear the clown. Nalivia decided acting the fool was how he managed to stay alive all these years with his brother in power. Nalivia recognized deep down that Boultori was anything but a fool, and he would prove it when he was king.

"Tomorrow, first light, we will be at the palace walls. One of you will break down the doors, probably Nalivia, since she has some experience with her talisman," Beir remarked.

Anarigar joined the conversation. "Nalivia can fly over the wall if need be. I mean, if you don't want our approach to be heard, she can fly over the wall and open the gates to the palace."

"Not a bad idea, but how will she manage the guards? The gate is also very heavy for such a little girl, even if she could unlatch it. I think we will stick with the idea of breaking it down and then meet the guards with swords if need be," Beir said.

"I don't like the idea of striking down the guards. Most of them are good men who are being forced into service by threats to their families. Maybe we could convince them to side with us," Boultori said, remembering the kindness showed to him while being held prisoner.

Beir did not respond immediately. He sat and thought for a minute. "I don't know if we can take the chance that the guards would side with us. They have been coerced for so long that it is second nature for them to do as commanded. If I thought for a moment that they would drop their weapons and return to their homes, I would go along with your idea, but I just don't think that is going to happen."

"We need to give them that chance, Beir. They are my people. What kind of a king would I be if I started out killing my own people? There has to be a way to free Rowanda and Emeraza that does not include killing." Boultori seemed almost depressed as he sat making plans.

The nomad spoke up for the first time, "I agree with Boultori. I know most people in the city live in fear of King Nashua. Once they see Boultori is here to take power from his brother, most of the people will support him. I believe that extends to the guards as well. Giving them a chance to side with the new king will benefit everyone. Those who do not will show their intentions immediately. Then we can counteract them with the necessary force."

"What about when your tribe returns in the morning? Won't they attack the gates and kill the guards?" Beir asked in earnest.

"I will be at the city gate first thing in the morning. In fact, I will be there before the first light. The doors will be opened, and any guard that does not agree to join us will be dispatched," the nomad said.

"Brave talk, but I don't see how you will do that alone," Beir remarked.

With a smile on his face, the nomad said, "Who said I will be alone? I have many friends in this city. While you sleep here on my floor, I will be about the city rounding up trusted comrades. The gates will be opened for my tribe when your plan goes into effect. Don't be concerned about me. I will get the job done."

The nomad got to his feet. "No time like the present. You will be safe here for the night. My wife and children will be on guard all night long." With a bow and a graceful hand blessing to the group, the nomad left the house.

"I wish we could make this plan work without any violence. I know that some of the guards truly are loyal to the king. Not all the people in this city are good. Many of the guards enjoy the power they receive by being the king's men. We will meet with resistance. The fact that we will be giving warnings may not play well into our hands. It will only give the king and his men time to cause harm," Beir said sorrowfully.

With their heads together, the band sat up into the quiet hours of the night, refining their plan. First, Nalivia nodded off and then Anarigar. Boultori and Beir decided they, too, should get some sleep. Dawn was only a few hours away, and it would be better to be somewhat rested than exhausted when Boultori used his magic for the first time.

CHAPTER SIXTEEN

 Rowanda sat in the kennel amongst the krerri. She loved the touch of their soft fur. She even loved their smell. She had asked Emeraza if she could take one home to Neslora when they opened a confluence. Emeraza emphatically told her, 'No!'

"I just want a pet, Grandmother. I think a krerri would make a perfect pet. See how soft they are and listen to the purr. It makes a person happy just to hear that noise," Rowanda argued.

Emeraza, sitting apart from the krerri, with distrust in her eyes, replied, "Those animals are meant to be wild. It is a shame anyone would confine them up in a small kennel and only take them out to hunt. It just is not natural. It would not be natural for one of them to sleep at your feet in your bedroom either."

"I suppose you are right," Rowanda said as she continued to stroke one of the krerri's head.

Rowanda became concerned. "Grandmother, if Boultori is able to make Arolsen a lush, green world like Neslora, what will become of the desert creatures? Can they adapt and live in a forest?"

"I don't know, child. Maybe when Boultori is king, he can make a huge desert reserve for the creatures to live in happily and unmolested. It would be nice if the animals could live in peace and not be hunted or subjected as the krerri have been. We will talk to

Boultori. I am sure he will be able to make a park with a water source for them. It should be as natural as the desert is at present so the creatures can go about being what they were intended to be."

Rowanda daydreamed about a large desert park where her new friends could roam and go about their business as wild creatures. She liked the idea of the people of Arolsen having what they needed to be happy without causing harm to the animals of the region. Solutions were possible when someone wanted the best for everyone. Rowanda knew Boultori was kind and would work to make everyone happy.

The first thing was for the king to be overthrown. Rowanda had no idea where Beir was and whether he knew where she and Emeraza were being held. She also wondered whether the nomads had found Boultori and what Nalivia and Anarigar discovered on their trek. Everything was unsure at the moment. All she knew for sure was that Emeraza's powers were not suspected by the king, or she would be in a jail cell at this very moment.

Rowanda's mind on future events, she asked Emeraza, "Grandmother, what do you think the king has planned for tomorrow? He said something about a hunt. Does that mean I need to go with the krerri? What will happen to you?"

"I doubt the king will want an old lady along, but somehow we must not be separated. I think I will be allowed to stay with you if the krerri put themselves between the guards and myself. Do you think you can communicate to the krerri that they must keep the guards from approaching me?" Emeraza asked the young girl.

Rowanda nodded, "Of course, the krerri will do as I wish. They will surround you and not let any guard near you, but what happens if the king intervenes. We have not seen his full powers. We just saw what he did to that poor guard without even touching him. He could do the same thing to me or you or even the krerri. I would imagine the king would decide to kill all the krerri if it suited him."

"That is a problem for tomorrow. Right now, we need to sleep. I have a feeling we are going to need all our strength in the morning."

Suddenly startled, Rowanda heard the jingling of keys and the lock being opened from the other side of the door. Instantly the krerri got to their feet and started to pace and growl.

"It is morning, and the king is ready for the hunt. I have brought you and the old lady a small meal to start the day. Be ready when the next guard comes to fetch you," the man said, not unkindly.

"I want my grandmother to come with me. I don't want to go alone with the king and his hunting party," Rowanda said shyly to the man as he retreated.

Looking back at Rowanda as he opened the door slightly, the guard looked sadly down at the child. "I am afraid I can do nothing for you. The king decides everything. If he says your grandmother may accompany you, then she can. If not, she will need to stay in this cell. I will mention your request to the king's aide, though."

Leaving the women to eat, the door was closed and locked. Emeraza watched and listened to the exchange but did not say a word while the guard was present.

"If the king does not agree to your request, this may be the only time that we can escape. I don't like the idea of leaving your father in Arolsen again, especially since we have not gained the chalice and pouch for which we came, but I won't allow the king to separate us. I will open a confluence, and we will return to Neslora. From the other side, I will decide when and where to re-enter this world to find your father, Nalivia and your talisman," Emeraza said in her no-nonsense demeanor.

Rowanda was about to object when two guards entered the kennel. Barely cracking the kennel door, they asked Rowanda to make sure the krerri were under control before opening the door wider. When the krerri went to the side of the child and the old lady, circling them, the guards opened the door warily.

"Please follow me," the one guard said politely. The other guard remained in the rear and followed at what he thought was a safe distance. The lead guard tried hard to not look back to see if he was being stalked. Squaring his shoulders and working hard to act bravely, he walked down the hallway that led out to the courtyard.

The sun was amazingly bright, even though it was barely past dawn. The chill of the desert night was warming, and it promised to be another hot day. Rowanda looked around the courtyard. It was luxurious with plants to the point that it almost felt like a tropical forest. Rowanda realized King Nashua's greed extended to even his plants. There was no planning or care as to where each shrubbery and flowers were planted. Each plant encroached on the other, and Rowanda knew that soon the plants would strangle each other and the courtyard would be an abandoned garden with little appeal to anyone. Rowanda noticed Emeraza was looking forlornly at the courtyard as well. Probably thinking the same thought.

Outside the gate of the courtyard, King Nashua was mounted on his horse, with several of his most trusted guards in attendance. "How are my krerri this morning, little girl? Are they fit and ready for the hunt? I released several prisoners into the desert last night, and I am anxious to hunt them down. My krerri know what to do, but I didn't think you would know what is expected of you."

Appalled, Rowanda brazenly said, "We are hunting men?"

"Of course, men, women, and a child or two. What did you think? You really did not think this was going to be a lizard hunt, did you? What would I want with lizards?" Booming into laughter, Rowanda noticed his men joined in gleefully.

"That is evil!" Rowanda yelled as Emeraza came forward and put her hand on Rowanda's shoulders to calm her.

Whispering, Emeraza said, "Be still, child. This is not the time to make the king mad. We don't know his powers."

Rowanda relaxed her stance but continued to seethe in her heart. She turned her face into her grandmother's robe and cried at the horror of what the king intended to do.

The king continued laughing said, "It is nice your grandmother has sense. I will allow her to accompany us on this hunt if it keeps your tongue in your mouth. You are lucky I did not strike you down for the disrespect you just showed me. Guards, give the old lady a horse to ride. The girl will stay on foot with the krerri."

Dragging Emeraza to a waiting horse, Rowanda's grandmother had no time to object to Rowanda being on foot. Hoisted up on the back of a horse, Emeraza took the reins and was surrounded by guards as the company headed out of the gate with the krerri and Rowanda at the front.

As the day heated, Rowanda found herself struggling on foot. The krerri huddled close to her so that she could lean on them. Feeling dizzy from heat and fatigue, one krerri dropped to the ground and laid at her feet. Rowanda knew the big cat was offering her a ride.

"The king clapped his hands appreciatively and bellowed, "Now that is what I call a kennel master. Look at how the animals serve her. I need to know how she does that."

Emeraza sat upon her mount and watched the king constantly. She searched his person to see what charms were visible. Only seeing his sword and wand in the king's belt, Emeraza had no way of knowing what other charms the king had until he chose to use them.

A shout from one of the guards let the king know there were some people on the horizon. The king's face lit up with a horrible contortion of wicked glee. "Now the fun begins," he said.

Rowanda shaded her eyes and strained to see what the guard had spotted. Barely visible in the far distance was a woman and her child, struggling to ascend a sandhill. Rowanda's heart sank. There was no way she would command the krerri to attack. Suddenly she understood why the king had allowed Emeraza to come on the hunt. It would either be the woman and her child who died, or her grandmother.

CHAPTER SEVENTEEN

Beir quietly woke his sleeping companions. "I think we'd best be going. We need to survey the gates to the palace while it is still early. I would like to wait until we know the nomads are at the city gates to enter the palace, but we need to know how many guards are on duty. It is better to have firsthand intelligence and knowledge than to go in blind."

Nalivia and Anarigar both sat up, rubbing the sleep from their eyes. Boultori just yawned and shook his head in agreement as the door opened and the lady of the house entered with food and beverages. Beir thanked her graciously and wondered if she had slept at all.

Boultori rose to assist the nomad's wife with the tray as the same little girl stood behind her mother with a tray of cups. Boultori smiled at the little girl and took the tray from her small hands. "Your parents must be very proud of you. Not only are you as beautiful as the evening stars, but you are also very helpful to your mother. Your parents are blessed to have so many delightful children."

The little girl just giggled. No one had compared her to evening stars before, and she loved the comparison. "Which evening star do I look like?" She asked softly.

"Why the brightest and the best one," was Boultori's immediate answer. "Tonight, look to the sky, and you will see one far brighter than the others. It will twinkle brilliantly in the sky. That is the one you remind me of the most."

The girl's mother beamed at the compliment for her youngest child and smiled, thanking Boultori for his kindness as she ushered the child from the room, leaving her company to eat and finish their last-minute planning.

While filling their stomachs with food and water, Beir reiterated what each would do once they left the home of the nomad's family. After taking inventory of their charms and weapons, Beir announced it was time to go.

Few people were on the streets at this early hour; however, storekeepers and vendors were starting to move about to begin their workday. Nalivia kept her hood over her head and stayed close to Anarigar, never looking directly at the men they passed in the streets and alleys.

If people recognized Boultori, no one shouted out a greeting or let their eyes meet his. Trying to remain anonymous was key to the plan. Only the people gathered by the nomad to confront the guards at the gate should be aware of Boultori's presence in the city. Most knew that Boultori escaped prison by word of mouth. The city knew something was about to happen, but it was best to act as normal as possible for fear of the king and his men.

Beir knew spies would be out on the streets. How many of the storekeepers or vendors were spies pretending to be honest city dwellers and how many of them were hired by the king was yet to be known. It was possible that all the people on the streets were spies looking for Boultori, but Beir doubted that to be the case. It was more likely that most of the men encountered were just honest men trying to make a living.

Rounding the corner into an alley leading closer to the palace walls, Beir was quickly stopped by a man who was hiding against the wall of a building. "You are Beirimor, am I right?" he asked. "I have news for you concerning your daughter and mother."

Shocked, he was recognized by this man and that he even knew about Rowanda and Emeraza made Beir stop in his tracks. "How do you know about my daughter and mother?"

"I just saw them; I served them breakfast. Your daughter asked me to make sure that her grandmother could attend her on the hunt this morning. I made sure the king's aide would allow your mother to go with your daughter," the man said.

"You mean Rowanda and my mother are not in the palace?" With suspicion, Beir continued his inquiry, "Why would you want to help us?" Beir asked the man as he crowded closer to him, keeping to the shadows of the dark and narrow alley.

The rest of the group also crowded into the alley to hear what the man needed to say. Boultori immediately recognized the man and embraced him. "Ter'ish, my friend, how are you?" Looking to Beir, he added, "This man can be trusted above all others. He is like a brother to me. Listen to him carefully. He will have all the knowledge we need to know."

"You flatter me, Boultori. I am but your faithful servant and not a fountain of knowledge as you supposed," Ter'ish said good-naturedly.

"Tell us what you know. Is there a safer place than this alley, or did you pick it because it was as safe as any other place? How did you know we would be coming this way?" Boultori asked curiously.

Ter'ish answered, "Your nomad friends are friends of mine. When the word was spread that all who are against King Nashua should be on alert today, I was leaving the palace after working there all night. Word came that you and a group of friends had arrived to overthrow the king. I knew the girl and old woman were special, and in a moment of brilliance, I knew who they were and how important they were to the cause. I believe that King Nashua also is suspicious of them as well."

"Do you know where they are?" Beir asked anxiously.

"King Nashua knows your daughter has special control over the krerri. He took her out in the desert to hunt prisoners. He wanted to see if he could control her better than she can control the krerri. He is always looking for more weapons. I believe he feels that he could amass an army of krerri to keep any revolution at hand. His spies told him that something is starting to happen in the palace city. Capturing more krerri and having them roam the streets would strike fear into any person siding with the revolutionists. I doubt that King Nashua knows who Rowanda might be," Ter'ish told the group.

"We need for the king to return from the desert now. The nomads will be at the gate soon. We plan to strike down the palace gates as the nomad flood in through the city gates. With the repressed city dwellers joining us, we felt we had a chance to overthrow King Nashua, but he needs to be here for the plan to happen," Boultori complained.

"I will return to the palace and shout that the nomads are about to attack the gates. The guards will send word to King Nashua immediately, and he will return. King Nashua believes he is the only one who can control this world, and he will return quickly," Ter'ish remarked. "I will go now."

Watching his friend running down the alley towards the palace gates, Boultori turned to Beir. "Do we wait and give him time to raise the alarm, or do we follow and attack on his heels?"

Beir thought for only a moment. "We wait until we see a rider leave, knowing he will go straight to the king, and then we will start our plan. There should be plenty of chaos when the nomads attack the main city gates. I doubt we will miss the fact of their arrival. So, in the meantime, we will stay here in the shadows. I have a feeling, it will only be a short time before we put our plan into action."

Watching from a safe distance, Anarigar announced that a rider was dispatched from the palace and was riding swiftly into the desert. He was sure Ter'ish had alerted the palace guards, and the king would soon return.

"It is best that we are in the palace before King Nashua returns. I want to know how many of the guards are with us and how many of the guards will need to be dispatched," Beir stated.

"That means we should go to the palace gate. Maybe Ter'ish will make it easy for us and have the deserters to King Nashua ready to fight the loyalists. It would be nice to be able to walk right through the gates and declare the palace as the property of King Boultori." Anarigar said.

"King Boultori. That does sound nice, doesn't it?" laughed Boultori. "Anarigar will be my chief adviser."

Anarigar puffed with pride. "I will be whatever you want me to be. I will even be the shepherd of your goat herd if that pleases you."

Everyone chuckled at Anarigar's statement. "Just keep your blue gem close to your heart. We have not overthrown the king yet. There are too many unknowns waiting for us. I hear King Nashua is a powerful wizard. He is not going to give up power just because Boultori claims the throne," Nalivia said, breaking the jovial mood.

Once again, quiet and reflective, the group moved closer to observe the palace gates. Nalivia spoke again, "I think Anarigar was correct when he said I should fly over the walls. I could spy to see what is happening with the guards. It would be good to know if we will be greeted with cheers or spears."

"I don't feel good about sending a girl into the palace by herself. What if you are captured? You could even be killed if a guard sees you flying and mistakes you for a witch. Witches are not tolerated here. I am almost surprised that King Nashua did not announce that Rowanda was a witch when he saw her abilities with the krerri. Wizards do not want disruption to their power, and a powerful witch would be more than a disruption," Beir remarked with concern in his voice.

"I am going," Nalivia announced. "I will go around to the back and fly over where no one will notice me. Once inside, I will look like a serving girl and nothing more. No one will even notice me, let alone stop me. I know I can do this."

Boultori nodded and said, "I think she is right. If Nalivia could see if my brother's loyal guards are disarmed, it would benefit all of us. I have no desire to strike down anyone, even those loyal to my brother. I believe that most of them will be relieved to have my brother out of power. They will come around and join us if given some time to think about it. I would like to give them that time and not make their wives widows and their children fatherless. Killing them would only breed more enemies as their sons grow up to want to avenge their fathers."

Not liking the idea of Nalivia going into the palace alone, Beir said, "Alright, you making a valid point, Boultori, but I don't want Nalivia to go in alone." Turning to Anarigar, Beir continued, "You said that Nalivia carried you up in the air when you needed to get over the boulder. Would you be willing to go with Nalivia if she can carry you once again?"

Anarigar took Nalivia's hand. "I would gladly go with Nalivia to spy and to protect her."

Nalivia blushed. "What are we waiting for? Let's go. The sooner we take flight, the sooner we will be able to report what is going on inside the palace."

Feeling inside her pouch, Nalivia touched the Bumblebee's wing that represented air. She carried Anarigar once before, she had no doubts that she could carry him over the palace wall. Holding onto Anarigar's hand and running down the alley, Beir did not have a chance to wish them 'good luck.' He wished the children did not need to be involved, but he counted on Nalivia and Anarigar.

CHAPTER EIGHTEEN

 King Nashua leered at Rowanda. He was enjoying her objections to harming the woman and her child. He could see from the fear in her eyes that she already realized she would need to make a decision to save her grandmother if she disobeyed. Having so much power over other people's lives was pleasing. King Nashua relished his command over life and death.

"Are you ready to send the krerri to attack the woman and her child? Or would you rather watch as I destroy your grandmother slowly and painfully?" King Nashua said, never letting his eyes leave Rowanda's.

"If you decide to let your grandmother suffer and refuse to send out the krerri, just know that I will send my guards to kill the escaped prisoners anyway. What will it be? Your decision. You can save your grandmother by doing as I command or all three of them die," King Nashua said casually.

Rowanda looked to her grandmother for help. She could not allow her grandmother to die a slow and painful death, but she could not send her krerri to kill the helpless woman and her child either. There was no winning.

Rowanda started to let her hand go under her cloak, but with a warning shake of her head, Emeraza stopped her. The wizard was watching too intently, and he would see her reach for her charms. At this point, no one had searched either her or Rowanda. Their only hope depended on keeping their talisman secret. If King Nashua discovered their charms, all would be lost.

"Well..." King Nashua said once again in his irritatingly calm voice, "What is it going to be? Are you going to do as I command, or am I going to need to show you just how powerful I am before you are willing to obey? You will soon realize that you are now working for me. There is no reason why you should delay it. All is lost. You are a tool for me to use as I wish to use you. The krerri are under your control, but you are under my control. I have great plans for the krerri, and you are the key. You can make this easy, or you can make this hard."

"If I am a tool, I don't understand why you need to kill those innocent people just to make me realize what I am. I concede that I am a tool, so why not let the woman and her child live?" Rowanda asked, hoping the king would be merciful.

"I will kill them...because I can. It is just that plain and simple. Those slaves don't serve any purpose. It is not like either of them can do anything that benefits me. Why do I want to feed them? They cost me money. They only exist for my pleasure. My pleasure right now is the hunt and watching my krerri kill them."

Rowanda racked her brain, trying to think of another angle that might save the woman and her child. She wondered if Emeraza might be able to do something...anything...to get the king's attention away from her long enough for her to gather her charms and work some magic—any magic that might save the two people who barely made it to the top of the dune. Getting out of sight of the hunting party in no way made it safer for them. Something momentous would need to happen to save them now. Rowanda was aware there were more prisoners out in the desert that King Nashua intended to hunt and kill. These two were only the first to be encountered. The thought that the day would continue with her being forced to kill one person after another made her so sick to her stomach that she vomited the entire contents onto the desert sand.

"Oh, dear, the child is sick," mocked the king. All his guards laughed at his remark. "What should we do. Maybe she needs some water. Get down off your horse and give her a drink," commanded the king to one of his closest guards.

Slowly, the guard dismounted, retrieving his flask of water from his belt. He watched the krerri as he walked closer, noting the hackles on their back rise as he moved towards the girl.

"Hurry up! Give the girl some water," the king taunted. A sparkle in his eyes stirred the guard forward. The guard knew he was either going to be killed by the krerri or the king if he made a mistake.

Rowanda saw his distress. A calming word to the krerri allowed the guard to come to her side. He handed her the flask, and she took it. Not waiting for her to return the flask, the guard moved away and back to his mount, never letting his eyes leave the krerri.

"There now, don't you feel better?" King Nashua said with ingenuous concern. "I know from experience that one must wash out one's mouth after vomiting. The taste is just vile. Now…where were we?"

The vomiting had not been a stalling mechanism. If it had been, Rowanda would have willed herself to vomit all day, but there was nothing left in her stomach to heave. Once more, she looked to Emeraza, hoping the older and wiser woman would indicate what she should do next.

"Get the old lady off the horse. I think the child needs a little demonstration as to what I will do to her grandmother if she stalls any longer," barked the king.

Two guards dismounted and went to Emeraza, where they pulled her from her horse allowing the old lady to land on her hip. Wincing, but not letting a word escape her mouth, Emeraza lay on the desert ground waiting to take anything the king might inflict on her if it would stall the death of the escaping prisoners.

Pulling out his wand, King Nashua glared at Emeraza. "What should I do first? I could cripple her and leave her in the desert to die, or maybe I should just pour water all over her and allow the terpor or wetchels to consume her." The king playfully sat on his horse and pretended to think long and hard. "No, that would be too cruel, even for me. I think causing agonizing pain might be enough to bring the child around. What do you think?" He said, playing up to his guards.

The guards knew better than to answer. They just laughed and encouraged the king to continue his terrible game.

Looking up, a horseman could be seen coming in the distance from the direction of the palace. As he got closer, one could see the horse was drenched in white, frothy foam from the exertion of running in the hot desert sun.

"What could this be?" asked the king out loud. Watching as the guard came closer, the other guards moved their horses so that the approaching man could come close to the king. It was apparent that something was amiss.

As the horse came to a stop, Rowanda watched the poor animal heaving from the exertion of running all morning in the blazing sun. She felt pity for the animal and wished she could do something for its distress. She wondered if the horse had enough energy to make it back to the palace. Her thoughts of the horse stopped as she heard what the guard was saying to the king.

"Your Highness, I have word that the nomads are attacking the gates. I rode as fast as I could to find you. We have no hope of stopping them from sacking the city without your power. I humbly ask that you return and intervene," the guard said without once looking at the king's face.

Gathering the reins to his horse, the king shouted commands, "One of you grab the girl and put her on the back of your horse. Two of you are to go and find the remaining prisoners and kill them. The rest of you follow me!"

Rowanda was swept up behind a guard with the krerri growling their displeasure but following immediately behind the girl who was now on horseback. Rowanda saw the two guards who were heading in the direction of the woman and her child. Taking the tooth from her pouch, Rowanda reached out to any terpor in the area to come and protect the fleeing prisoners. Rowanda knew the two guards would be stopped in their tracks at any moment. Smiling, Rowanda allowed herself some pleasure in knowing she had just saved several people.

The exhausted horse and its rider tried to keep up with the other horses now returning at full gallop towards the palace. Knowing the animal needed rest and the guard would continue to whip him until the horse dropped dead, Rowanda channeled her energies into forming a small whirlwind blocking that horse from the group. Looking over her shoulder, she saw the horse rear in fright, knocking the guard to the ground where he lay immobile. Figuring that he was knocked out, but probably not seriously hurt, Rowanda was relieved that the horse could stand and catch its breath. Hopefully, the horse would wander away and not be available to the guard when he regained consciousness. Both would be saved in the long run.

Seeing the palace in the distance, Rowanda watched as the tiny wall grew more significant as they got closer and closer. Soon the beautiful designs on the wall were clearly defined, and she knew something momentous would be happening soon.

Rowanda wished she also had her chalice and pouch of seeds with her other charms so she could achieve her ultimate power-- Parados. Knowing Emeraza was no match for King Nashua, Parados would be the only way King Nashua would be overthrown. The future of both worlds weighed Rowanda down as the back gates of the palace opened to receive them.

CHAPTER NINETEEN

 Nalivia and Anarigar ran around to the side of the palace walls out of sight from prying eyes. Stopping and looking around to make sure no one would see them, Nalivia grasped her Bumblebee's wing in her hand.

"Just like before, Anarigar, I need for you to close your eyes and empty your mind. I can't have any of your thoughts weighing us down. Can you do that again?" Nalivia asked.

"I can do an even better job this time. I promise I won't open my eyes to peek until we are safely on the ground, and you tell me when to open them," Anarigar announced remembering the fall he took when he peeked while in midair. The thought of hitting the ground as hard as he had done before made him determined to do better.

Nalivia smiled, remembering as well. "Good. I can use all the help possible in this. I have not mastered any of my charms yet, so cross your fingers, close your eyes and empty your mind."

"Why did you feel you needed to remind me you have not mastered your charms yet. How am I supposed to empty my mind now?" Anarigar complained.

"Just do it!" snapped Nalivia as she grasped Anarigar's hand and closed her own eyes. As before, Anarigar felt the wind lift him into the air. He kept his eyes closed tight as promised and started a chant in his head, "Empty my mind, empty my mind, empty my mind." Feeling scraping on his sandals, Anarigar knew Nalivia had barely cleared the top of the wall. He hoped Nalivia would not drop him down the side of the wall, scraping skin as he descended, but he kept his eyes closed, not wanting to see anything bad happening.

With a thump, Anarigar felt his feet touch the ground. "Can I open my eyes?"

Nalivia giggled, "I did it! We are safely on the other side of the wall. I just don't know exactly where we are and how to get to the courtyard at the front gate. I guess we will just need to explore."

Anarigar felt giddy as well. He had landed on his feet. All his skin was still attached to his body. Amazed and in good spirits, Nalivia grabbed his hand and said, "Let's try this direction."

Knowing boys and girls did not hold hands in the palace city, Anarigar released her hand. "I will lead. It will look less suspicious if you follow me with your eyes downcast. You know it would not be proper for you to hold my hand in public here."

Nalivia agreed and let Anarigar lead the way. He followed along the wall until he found a path that looked as if it might lead towards the main gate. As he walked along, he saw several women working industriously doing laundry. Not wanting to stare or draw attention to themselves, Anarigar just glanced in their direction. Stopping in mid-step, Anarigar got a strange feeling in the pit of his stomach. One of the washwomen looked oddly familiar. He searched his memory for why this one woman would catch his attention.

"Why did you stop so abruptly, Anarigar? Are there guards blocking our way?" Nalivia whispered as she drew closer behind Anarigar.

"I'm sorry. It is probably nothing, but that one woman with the green headscarf seems familiar to me, and I don't know why," Anarigar whispered back.

"This is no time to try to figure out why a woman looks familiar. Just keep moving before anyone takes notice of us. We have a job to do," Nalivia said as she nudged the boy forward.

Keeping his eyes straight ahead and not glancing at the women, Anarigar and Nalivia was just abreast of the group of washwomen when a strangled gasp escaped one of the women.

"Anarigar, is that you?" one of the women said as she started to get to her feet.

Anarigar inspected the face of the woman with the green headscarf. Years melted away as he recognized her now. "Mother!"

Just as Anarigar started to break into a run to get to his mother, a shout could be heard from a man standing on the other side of the women doing laundry. Cracking his whip, he could be heard to say, "Get back to work, you lazy drometarius. If I need to come down there, I will beat you senseless. You two kids, move along!"

Anarigar whispered as Nalivia dragged him onward, "I will be back for you, Mother." Tears ran down his cheeks as the two children moved towards the courtyard. Whether tears of joy or sadness, Nalivia could not discern.

Once around the corner, Nalivia stopped. "Anarigar, that was your mother? You said she was taken as a slave. You must be overjoyed to know she is alive, and we will be able to rescue her as soon as King Nashua is overthrown."

"All these years without my mother and she has been working like a slave. If that guard ever laid a whip on her, he will need to answer to me!" Anarigar said as he touched his blue gem. Brilliant blue light streamed through his fingers as he spoke his threat.

"Anarigar! Your gem is responding to you. You do have powers. I wonder what they will be...just be careful until you know how to use the gem," Nalivia cautioned. "We need to keep moving. I have a strange feeling, things are going to happen quickly now. We must get to the courtyard."

Walking around another corner, Nalivia and Anarigar slowed their steps. Guards were running through the courtyard in disarray. It seemed they were moving at odds with each other. Observing, Anarigar realized they were forming sides. Ter'ish was standing close to the gates, and many of the guards were moving to side with him while others were forming a battle line opposite them.

Anarigar grabbed Nalivia, and they took cover behind a wagon filled with many barrels stacked one upon the other. Crouching down, out of sight, the two children waited to see what was happening.

Ter'ish shouted to the opposing men, "This is your only chance to overthrow that dictator, King Nashua. It is now or never! You know he is evil, but we have help now. The nomads are with us, most of the city dwellers are with us. We have support from another world. You cannot win. Don't be stupid and side with the wizard. Join us and make Boultori our king!

On the opposite side, men looked to their left and right. Each was trying to size up what the other was thinking. When one bolted to join Ter'ish, several more ran with him. They were met with jeers from the line they had deserted. "Traitors! Cowards! Sons of Drometarius!"

Even with threatening slurs being thrown at the men, even more, rushed from the lines to join Ter'ish. Soon only twenty men held their line in support of King Nashua. Realizing how out-numbered they were, the loyalist rushed back to the palace to secure the throne for their king.

Cheers went up as Ter'ish flung the gates open, allowing Boultori to enter the palace. "King Boultori! King Boultori! Long live King Boultori!"

People filled the streets, and singing was heard from side alleys and rooftops. Nomads riding camels were seen coming from the main gates, and Beir knew the nomads had entered the city with the help of the revolutionists inside the city walls.

Anarigar told Nalivia to rush back to Beir. "I must go back to my mother,' and off Anarigar ran. Nalivia did as instructed and rushed to meet Beir.

The back gates opened, and the loyal guards waited as King Nashua entered the palace. Each thought how King Nashua would destroy the army which threatened his kingdom. Waiting for orders, King Nashua angrily told his guards to bring the girl and the old woman to his throne room as he dismounted and stormed in that direction.

Dragging Emeraza and Rowanda to the throne room, the guards stood ready to do as commanded. Flinging the doors open to the balcony above the courtyard, King Nashua summoned the guards to bring his prisoners onto the balcony beside him. Grabbing Rowanda by the throat, he bellowed to the crowd below.

"Boultori! You dare to threaten my rule over this world," Nashua continued, "come up to my throne room, or I will cast this little witch down at your feet!"

Pulling Rowanda off her feet by her throat, Rowanda felt lightheaded as she struggled to breathe. Emeraza reached for her whirligig and lifted Rowanda out of King Nashua's grasp. Spinning her up and out of his reach, she brought the child down to her side.

"Old woman, I see you are a sorceress, but you are no match for me. Let's see what you have in your arsenal," the king said with a sneer.

Drawing out his wand, King Nashua slammed Emeraza into the far wall where she hit her head and dropped to the floor. Moving slowly to her feet, Emeraza formed a puff of smoke in her hands. Laughing, the king said, "Is that all you have, old woman?" Just as Emeraza released a fireball directed toward the smiling king.

In a flick of the wrist, King Nashua sent a shield to block the fireball, directing it back at the old lady. Seeing Emeraza struggling to find her piece of coral to create a water wall, Rowanda's sword sent a flurry of air to extinguish the fireball back into its original puff of smoke.

"Another little witch! So that is why the krerri love you. You enchanted them. You know what we do with witches in this world, don't you? We burn them at the stake," King Nashua said as he directed his wand at Rowanda.

Boultori, Nalivia, and Beir rushed into the throne room, pushing past the guards. With spears ready, the guards threatened to harm the trio, but King Nashua halted them with one word. "Stop! I will handle all of my enemies. You can stand by and be entertained."

The guards stepped back to their positions and lowered their spears. Smiles cross their faces as they prepared for the show their king would put on.

"Welcome, brother. I made a mistake to underestimate your desire to be king. I allowed you to be the court jester. I thought that was what you really wanted to be. You were so convincing at being a fool. Let's see what you really have, shall we?" King Nashua said as he concentrated his anger towards his sibling.

Boultori pushed Beir aside. Hesitating for only a few seconds, Beir and Nalivia rushed towards Rowanda and Emeraza as Boultori pushed up his sleeves and prepared to battle his brother. All eyes bounced between King Nashua and Boultori.

King Nashua sneered. Boultori undecided which charm to try, let his hand fall upon his petrified bat. A gust of wind blew towards his brother, who laughed out loud and pretended fear.

"Oh, please, don't blow your stinky breath at me. I am so afraid!" King Nashua laughed, and suddenly all glee left his face as he pointed his wand at the oncoming wind, turning it into a flock of blackbirds flying straight towards Boultori's face.

Boultori waved his arms frantically to protect himself from the wings and beaks of the vicious birds. King Nashua bent over, laughing. The laughter continued as Boultori jumped from foot to foot, twirling in circles, trying hard to fend off the winged creatures.

Rowanda reached into her belt and allowed a touch of her hand on her sword. Thinking whirlwind, a twirling, whirling wind swooped the birds and carried them out of the balcony door opening.

"Brother, you really must learn to use your magic and not need to depend on a little girl to rescue you. That is just pathetic!"

Red rushed to Boultori's face. Embarrassed and humiliated for years by his older brother, Boultori grabbed his diamond, and a flash of angry red fire pulsed towards the evil king. Not stopping after one pulse, Boultori shot blast after blast of flames.

Taken by surprise for only a second, King Nashua barely got his wand in place to block each fiery ball. As each sweltering blast arrived, King Nashua's wand met each with ice. Sizzling sounds and steam filled the air.

Boultori grabbed his dowsing rod and using it and his diamond; jets of hot steam sprayed directly at his brother. The hot steam was met by an umbrella that directed the scorching vapors in all directions but leaving the king unharmed.

Tiring of the little game, King Nashua stood tall and aimed his wand directly at the group gathered with Emeraza. Seeing that King Nashua intended to divert his brother by harming his friends, Boultori grabbed the bone and caused a wall of vines to grow between his friends and the king.

While out of the view of the king, Emeraza hissed to Nalivia. "Where are Rowanda's chalice and seed pouch. She will need all of her powers to contend with the wizard. Does Boultori still have them?"

Nalivia's eyes brightened as she remembered that she held them on her person. Pulling them out from under her cloak, she passed the two charms to Rowanda.

King Nashua sent battleaxes to chip away at the vines. These tabars chipping away at the creepers, Boultori knew it was only a matter of time before the battleaxes would be hacking his friends to pieces. In desperation, Boultori held all his charms in his hands at one time and let his mind wrap around the entirety. Not knowing what would happen, Boultori decided any disaster was better than his friends being killed.

The room became silent as darkness slowly crept over the entire place. It spread like a fog, but so dense, nothing could be seen where it lay. It moved slowly across the room, stealing any noise as it covered the guards first and crept on towards the balcony.

The chopping sound stopped as the vine and axes succumbed to the darkness. The darkness threatened to cover the wizard as it spread out in all directions. Seeing the possible outcomes of the spreading darkness, King Nashua used his wand to create a giant dragon.

The dragon opened his mouth and breathed in the murky vapors, sucking them slowly into his gaping nostrils and cavernous jaws. The room slowly cleared of the menacing fumes, and once again, the king laughed with wicked glee.

The dragon eyed Boultori. Massive beyond belief, the scaly four-footed beast with its yellow snake eyes fixed on the little man. Moving cumbersomely forward, Boultori watched the dragon's approach. The front two legs stepped directionally forward as the two hind legs propelled the movement. Boultori knew if he injured the back legs, the speed forward would only be slowed, but if he could damage one of the directional front legs, the towering beast would need to change its direction.

Touching his charms, Boultori chose his dowsing rod once more. Pointing the divining olive branch at the dragon's left front leg, a large ice lance propelled itself into the dragon's leg. Howls of pain roared out of the injured beast. Infuriated, the dragon pushed on towards its intended victim but found itself limping slowly in circles to the left. Frustrated, the dragon increased his speed with his powerful hind legs and found itself spinning out of control.

Emeraza decided the moment was right. She did not want to wait to find out what horrific magic the king would use next. Boultori survived this far by his cleverness, a bit of luck, and no experience or skill.

"Rowanda, I have no magic left," Emeraza said. "The injury to my head has left me powerless. I will require time to recuperate, but we don't have time to waste. The king is getting increasingly angrier. I fear he is not going to continue to torment his brother much longer. I believe his next stroke of magic will be a killing one. It is time for you to summon all your powers to create Parados. I know you do not want to kill anyone, so I am suggesting we disarm the king, open a confluence and take him to Neslora, where he will be imprisoned for the rest of his natural life."

Looking to Nalivia, Emeraza asked, "Nalivia, how fast can you fly? I will need you to create confusion while Rowanda is opening the confluence. I also will need you to grab the king's wand if possible. If you don't think you can fly fast enough, I will need to think of something else. What do you say?"

Nalivia touched the element representing Air and found herself flying into the air. The dragon was spinning so fast that all eyes were on the creature as he seemingly grew smaller with each turn of his entire body. With one final spinning turn, the creature snapped out of sight; King Nashua turned his attention back to his brother.

"Excellent, Boultori," King Nashua growled. "I would never have expected you to use your brain. In fact, I was not aware you even had one. I tire of our little game. I fear it is time for you to die."

Boultori's eyes left his brother as he noticed Nalivia swooping down at his brother like a hummingbird. She darted quickly in one direction and then another, focusing her eyes on the wand.

King Nashua watched with interest, knowing the girl's magic was no match for his own. Pretending to swat at Nalivia as if she was a pesky fly, the guards joined the king in fits of laughter. When the king's laughter stopped, the guards quieted immediately.

"Little girl, this has been fun. I needed the comic relief, but now I tire of you. I am going to squash you like the bug you are," sniggered the king.

Gathering his wand in a show of power, exaggerating the pulling up of his sleeves to expose his wrists and forearms, King Nashua twirled his wand in his hands like a baton. Letting the wand slip through each finger until it rested gently in the palm of his hand, the king slowly followed Nalivia's flight. Pointing the tip of the wand at the young girl, the king was ready to act on his threat.

Nalivia continued to dart one direction and then another, trying to keep from being in the direct path of the wand. Seeing that her flittering was no match for the king's aim, Nalivia closed her eyes to her impending doom.

A horrific cracking noise caught the king's attention just before he was to discharge the force from his wand that would destroy Nalivia. A large gaping hole stood in the throne room's wall just behind Beir, Emeraza, and Rowanda. The confluence Rowanda created shimmered, allowing a glimpse of her world seeming like a desert mirage.

King Nashua felt the pull on his body. He knew he was being drawn into the confluence. In one defying moment, King Nashua flicked his wrist, directing the tip of his wand out of the balcony window just before Nalivia grabbed the wand from his hand. With no power, King Nashua was pulled into the hole where Beir was waiting to snatch him.

Emeraza stepped through the confluence as Nalivia flew into the hole. Emeraza told Rowanda to stepped through quickly. Just as Rowanda was about to enter, waving to Boultori, she heard screams from the people in the palace city. Seeing Boultori run to the balcony, Rowanda let the confluence snap closed with a brilliant spark of light. Running to Boultori's side, Rowanda saw the damage King Nashua managed to inflict with the last flick of his wand.

CHAPTER TWENTY

 Beir immediately grabbed Nashua. "You aren't king anymore! You will get what you deserve for your years of terror amongst the people of Arolsen. Forever locked away is how we will protect Arolsen and your brother," Beir said without sympathy. Beir remembered being in Nashua's prison and Nashua now being his prisoner seem poetic justice.

"Rowanda did not come through the confluence with us!" shouted Nalivia.

"Don't worry, dear," Emeraza said soothingly. "She still had a few things left to be done in Arolsen. She will return soon. In the meantime, we have things to do ourselves. First, we must create a strong cell for Nashua and provide loyal Neslorian guards to watch over him every moment. I also see you brought his wand into this world. That means my sister sorceresses and myself must find a way to destroy it. I don't think it can be used in this world, but the fact that we could use our charms in Arolsen might prove me wrong."

Taking the wand from Nalivia, Emeraza led the way home. Beir, having bound Nashua's arms behind him, pushed him forward to follow Nalivia and Emeraza.

A wicked smile formed on Nashua's face as he saw his wand pass from Nalivia to Emeraza. As long as his wand was in this world, Nashua knew he had a chance to regain his powers and to return to his station as ruler of Arolsen. There is no way he would allow his brother to beat him and remain the new king.

Coming into the village, people gathered to cheer the return of their Elder. The guards who had entered their world on command from King Nashua were living freely amongst the villagers. Some hissed when they saw their overthrown king. It had been long decided that the ones who wanted to return to Arolsen would be allowed to do so when Emeraza returned, and those who wished to stay in Neslora may do so as well.

Scanning the guards in the crowd of Neslorians, Nashua singled out one guard he knew to be completely loyal to him. With a meaningful look, the guard knew to stay quiet and not to react to his king being led to the prison awaiting him. There would be time for him to slip out at night and speak to Nashua through a barred window while the guard dozed.

Nashua felt more in control, knowing his wand was in this world, and so was one of his most loyal guards. Things were looking up and Nashua now dreamed of being king of two worlds. As powerful as he was, Nashua knew he could definitely control both worlds. A feeling of immense satisfaction was growing in his soul. Smiling at the thought of actually having a soul, Nashua knew he did not need a soul. He had power. That was better than a soul.

Beir noted the change in Nashua. He looked where Nashua was staring and saw one man in the crowd. He watched the look that passed between the two, and Beir knew to be watchful of that particular man. Beir was only too aware that not all the guards hated Nashua. Some embraced him as the real king. Beir decided that man may, in fact, be a supporter of the wicked and corrupt regime.

CHAPTER TWENTY-ONE

 Going out onto the balcony, Boultori and Rowanda stood side by side. Disbelief formed on both of their faces as they looked to the desert outside the city walls. Coming towards the palace city was an army. It was not just any army; the soldiers were made of sand. With each step forward, they grew larger and larger as they became engorged with the sand beneath their feet.

"What has your brother done?" Rowanda asked Boultori.

Not answering, Boultori just stood watching in amazement. The guards rushed to the window as well. None of the guards knew what to do once King Nashua vanished. Seeing the advancing menace, the guards dropped their spears and ran from the throne room.

"I guess we can't count on my brother's guards," Boultori said as he watched them flee the room.

"I doubt they could do anything against that army anyway," was Rowanda's remark.

Watching his people fleeing in panic, Boultori knew if he was going to be their king, he must act quickly. Lives were at stake. His people's lives and his city would be fully engulfed by sand, leaving no trace of the palace or his people.

"Any suggestions, Little Dragon?" Boultori asked, using his nickname for the little girl.

"I think we need to get to the city walls before the sand soldiers get through the gate," replied Rowanda. "We both can try to think of a plan as we ride there."

Running down the stairs and out into the courtyard, Boultori yelled for horses to be brought. His command was obeyed immediately by the revolutionists waiting to see which king would appear the victor. Cheering for King Boultori, the remaining palace guards fell in behind Boultori and Rowanda to meet the challenge before them.

Arriving at the palace city walls, the hoard of city people joined Boultori and Rowanda on the ramparts of the Barbican facing out to the advancing army. Panic was evident on all the faces of the people as they watched the advance of the growing force of sand people.

"The desert has always been a dangerous place to live, but it has been our home. It was unkind of my brother to make the desert the enemy," thought Boultori out loud.

"We will need to use the desert against the desert, then," said Rowanda with a flash of an idea. Summoning her powers over the desert creatures, the people on the rampart watched as terpor and wetchels appeared almost out of nowhere.

Terpors flipped through the air, diving into some of the sand soldiers causing large holes in their bodies. Sand shifted, and the soldiers dropped back into the desert, creating large mounds. More and more terpors appeared, and the crowd watched in amazement as sand soldiers continued to fall back to earth.

Wetchels whipped their tails at the feet of the advancing army, knocking their legs out from under them, causing them, too, to fall back into mounds of sand. Even working tirelessly, Rowanda noted that there were too many sand soldiers for the desert creatures to destroy.

"Something else will need to be done. My friends are making a dent, but only a small dent. There are too many sand soldiers for them to destroy alone," Rowanda said in exasperation.

Boultori realized Rowanda's efforts were helping, but she was right. There were too many soldiers advancing toward his city. Not only were there too many, but they increased in size with each step. Boultori thought a giant whirlwind may be the answer.

Summoning his petrified bat's power over the air, Boultori created a cyclone that whipped many of the advancing armies back out to the desert floor, but a large number of remaining soldiers kept coming.

Drawing on his dowsing rod, Boultori created a downpour drenching the sand army. Now heavy with water, the sand soldiers sunk under the weight of the water, creating large hills outside the city.

Fatigued, but seeing that water was the answer, Boultori tried hard to create more rainstorms to flush the backline of the army to the ground. When the dowsing rod failed with the last attempt, he asked Rowanda to assist.

Rowanda drew out her chalice and pouch of seeds. Flinging the seeds to the wind and spraying water from her chalice, the last row of advancing sand people fell to the desert floor, sodden with liquid and seeds. Immediately, sprouts erupted from the ground, and small plants pushed their way to the sun above.

Enlightened, Boultori hugged Rowanda. "You have done it again. You have created a vineyard. This time we will not need to burn them to hide your magic."

Watching the vines grow strong in minutes, Boultori sang as greenish flowers bloomed, and grapes appeared in clusters that the flowering plants left behind.

"We will celebrate our good fortune with grape juice and wine!" shouted Boultori to the cheering crowd.

The gates were opened in the Barbican, and people flooded out with baskets to gather the grapes. Singing and dancing were seen and heard throughout the palace city as relief renewed the spirit of the people.

Rowanda watched from on top of the rampart with joy at seeing the celebration that instantly erupted. The nomad women danced merrily with colorful scarves flowing gently above their heads as their hands moved gracefully around their bodies. The chieftain joined his men in dance with hard stomping steps, and exuberant leaps into the air. Children laughed and raced around their parents and shouts of praise broke out in unison for their new king. "Long live King Boultori, long live our king!"

Boultori, small in stature, grew larger than life with the admiration of his people. He swelled with pride knowing that he, with the help of Rowanda and his friends, had just ended the reign of a cruel and evil king. He found peace knowing that his people would live out their lives with abundance from the plants that he would provide.

Looking down, Boultori saw Anarigar in the crowd with his mother by his side. Beckoning Anarigar to come up the stairs to be by his side, he knew he would never be alone. Anarigar would fulfill his promise to be whatever he needed him to be. Right now, he needed an apprentice that would learn his magic as Boultori also learned his own. Together they would master the newfound art of wizardry.

Sitting in the throne room, after celebrating into the wee hours of the night, the small group of companions talked until dawn.

Rowanda knew she would need to open another confluence and return to Neslora, leaving Arolsen in capable hands, but first, she wanted to hear the stories.

Anarigar told of finding his mother while in the company of Nalivia. "I had not seen my mother for years. She was taken by nomads and sold into slavery. My father looked endlessly for the nomads who took her, but he never could find a trace of them or mother. All these years, she has been a washwoman for the king and his soldiers." Anarigar said as he took his mother's chaffed hands in his own. "She will never need to wash a stitch of clothes again if I have any say."

Anarigar's mother smiled warmly at her son. "It will be my pleasure to wash the clothes of my husband and sons once more. I will relish getting my old life back."

"Mother, you and father, as well as my brothers, will be welcome in the palace. Isn't that right, Boultori. I mean King Boultori," corrected Anarigar as he addressed his new king.

Always jovial, Boultori laughed. "King, that sounds so strange to my ears. You may always call me Boultori, Anarigar. You have earned your place by my side. I can't wait to see what powers you discover with your blue gem. And yes, your family is welcome to live in the palace forever."

Anarigar answered, "I did find the blue gem reacts to my anger. When the guard refused to let my mother come to me when I returned to her, I was fuming. The blue gem in my grasp, erupted with a blazing blue light that knocked the soldier off his feet with such force, that he didn't get back to his feet, but crawled away like the desert rat that he was. In fact, I am sure I saw a tail starting to form between his legs."

Boultori laughed in mirth at his mental picture of the soldier turning into a rat when he noticed that Anarigar was not laughing.

"Do you mean you think you really transformed that guard into a rat?"

Anarigar and his mother both nodded their heads with startled looks in their eyes. "I think I have found what the power of the blue gem might be. I think it can transform one thing into another. I fear what might happen before I learn how to control the power," Anarigar whispered into Boultori's ear.

Boultori roared with laughter. "I think you need to watch your anger. I sure don't want to be the king over desert rats."

Rowanda enjoyed seeing Boultori acting like himself. She remembered her distrust of the small man when she first came to Arolsen. She recalled how he put himself in danger just to find eggs for her as a gesture of apology for making her upset. She now loved to hear him call her Little Dragon, a nickname that used to make her mad. She was going to miss seeing him when she returned to her own world, but she felt wonderful knowing that Arolsen could flourish without affecting Neslora. Both sister worlds would thrive.

Getting to her feet, Rowanda yawned. "I must get back to Neslora. I am curious as to how they are handling your brother. I hope you never need to contend with him again. My one fear is that Nalivia inadvertently took his wand through the confluence as she flew through. I must find a way to destroy it when I return. I know Grandmother Emeraza will train me in the ways of sorcery if I am to be the Elder Sorceress someday. I suppose I had better return and start that training. I will leave you now, but if you ever need me, just whisper my name three times into the desert wind. I believe I will be able to hear you on the winds that blow ever so gently in my world."

Boultori rose to his feet. He embraced Rowanda and walked with her to the wall, where she created the confluence that took his wicked brother out of his world. "And you do the same. If ever I can be of service to you, just whisper my name three times. I will hear your voice in the purrs of the krerri, the whip of the wetchel's tail and the hiss of the terpor. I also promise to leave a large portion of Arolsen for your friends to live upon forever. In fact, the desert park will be forever named Little Dragon Reserve in honor of my Little Dragon."

With a grateful tear in her eye, Rowanda gathered all her charms, creating Parados and watched as a twinkle of light announced the opening of a confluence that would allow Rowanda to enter her own world. With one last hug for her dear friend, Rowanda stepped back into Neslora, listening to the snap as the confluence closed behind her. Greeting her was the chirping of birds and buzzing of bees. The fragrant aroma of flowers continuously in bloom drifted into her nostrils as she breathed in the wonderful scents of Neslora.

Seeing where she was, Rowanda took the path that would lead her to her home, her parents, her grandmothers, and her waiting duties as the youngest new Elder of the Order.

To be continued...*The Child Rowanda, Underworld, The Child Rowanda Series/Volume 3*

Carole Walker Carter

Starting life in a small town in Nebraska, Carole and her family frequently moved across the USA, Carole met many fascinating personalities that inspired characters for her many stories. With a vivid imagination, Carole expressed her love of story-telling in Children's Literature, Mystery, Science Fiction, and Fantasy books as platforms for her expressive writing.

Carole lives presently in the Pacific Northwest with her husband, Don, her childhood sweetheart and partner, their pet dogs, several chickens, and a few fish. Carole's career involved working with children from pre-school through high school, dealing with special needs, and "at-risk'" children as an Occupational Therapy Assistant and Educational Assistant.

Aztara, Mastel Kingdom, the prequel to the *Aztarian Series*, providing insight into the lore of the creatures on Aztara. Surtees, Science Rules, the first volume in the *Aztarian Series* describes the narcissistic protagonist that abused both Surtarians and Aztarians for his own personal needs. Aztara, A Galactic Love Story, is the first published book and the second volume in the *Aztarian Series.* Aztara, Secrets Revealed, the revolt where Aztarians take their planet back. Carole announced in the summer of 2017 a mystery book series, *Evers and McFarlan Detective Series*. Final Alumni, Shadowy Faces, and Nine Points of a Circle all are available today. Carole also started a *Fantasy Series* in the fall of 2017 for young people. Little Dragon is the first book in the *Child Rowanda Series*, Return to Arolsen, The Underworld, and the Dragon Princess. Please watch for additional volumes in the *Aztarian Series, Evers and McFarlan Detective Series, The Child Rowanda*, Series, and Carole's many children stories on her website www.walkercarter.com and www.amazon.com.

Aztara, The Mastel Kingdom

By
Carole Walker Carter

Aztara, The Mastel Kingdom, tells the background story of the mastels before entering into a bonding relationship with the miners of Aztara. The setting for this book is two generations before the plague that killed all the Aztarian women during the time frame for Vol II *Aztara, A Galactic Love Story.*

Idyllic as it might seem, the mastels are nomadic, dependent upon the weather and growing cycles for the food they eat.

The bond between the griswells and mastels seems destined to failure, until Morsian, an inventor from the eastern factory villages, creates a symbiotic relationship that will change everything on Aztara…forever.

Explore the early world of Aztara and enjoy Mastel's unique story. This book will be available on Amazon, Kindle, Nook, and Barnes & Noble in the winter of 2019/2020.

Surtees, Science Rules
By
Carole Walker Carter

Surtees, Science Rules is the First book in Aztarian Series. In Surtees, Science Rules, we discover how ruthless a utopian society can be when the ruling power is Scientists.

Ananaya's family are the Oligarchs in this society. His father and mother are obsessed with increasing longevity to keep their power and wealth. Ryndor, Ananaya's father, set up several of his senior scientists as the leaders of scientific research centers.

Hoygazor became the leader of the Astro-Scientists that travel the universe. Eyutho lead research into Marine Science. Doyfear founded the Agricultural research centers. Kaycee'na, wife of Ananaya, developed Neurochemistry research.

Ananaya's sinister plans will become known as he maneuvers his way through the Oligarchy.

This book will be available on Amazon, Kindle, Nook, and Barnes & Noble in the winter of 2019/2020

AZTARA, A Galactic Love Story
By
Carole Walker Carter

In AZTARA, A Galactic Love Story, the second book in the *Aztarian Series* centers on two main characters and their magical creatures that they share a unique bond. The two main characters are caught up in their own personal grief.

Shayla, an Earth woman, who finds life on Earth hardly worth living after being deceived by her husband, and having her only son die, is close to suicide.

Ty, having lived through a plague that killed all the females on his planet, finds refuge in his work, mining a mineral instrumental to all aspects of life on Aztara, including telepathy, longevity, and levitation.

Scientists from Surtees, a dying planet, relocate to Aztara to receive the benefits of phyrium. In their attempt to rebuild the Aztarian population, they import Earth women who carry a specific gene, the warrior gene, to mate with the Aztarian men.

The story is about finding love, trust, and internal strength as well as romance, intrigue, and thrills while the two main characters come to grips with a situation, not of their own choosing.

Find this book on Amazon, Kindle, Nook, and Barnes & Noble Now!!

AZTARA, Secrets Revealed
By
Carole Walker Carter

AZTARA, Secrets Revealed, the third book in the Aztarian Series, opens with Shayla's and Ty's love for their twins, Nayela and Kestle. Nayela, the only interspecies girl who communicates telepathically with a mastel, finds others her age calling her a freak. Kestle has his hands full with being a gang member.

A tragic event occurs that changes everything for Kestle. Self-banished to the Wildlands leaves Kestle bitter, depressed, and alone to deal with situations he has never encountered. Going deeper into the Wildlands, in search of food and water, brings Kestle to the dreaded Orange River. Saving a young runaway girl, Sinaka, from certain death, Kestle's loneliness ends, but he discovers there is more to this young girl than he first thought. Sinaka finds it is her turn to save Kestle when he is wounded by a monster. With unexpected help from a beautiful creature and Sinaka's psychic and empathic powers, Kestle finds healing.

The Surtarian Chief Scientist, Ananaya, accelerates his plan to genetically modify the Aztarian/Earthling boys' Warrior Genes, with performance-enhancing injections. Ananaya's plot is to create a daunting army of new Enforcers.

All hell breaks loose when the usually passive Aztarians decide to fight to get their boys back.

Find this book on Amazon, Kindle, Nook, and Barnes & Noble Now!!

Final Alumni
By
Carole Walker Carter

The Final Alumni is the first book in the *Evers and McFarlan Detective Series*. This series follows two high school best friends who join forces to solve multiple cases. Tish, haunted by a childhood experience, enables herself with many disciplines of martial arts, while Scotty falls back on his sharpshooter training and physical prowess as a football hero. Together they make an unstoppable team.

Now living in Chicago, Illinois, and mentored by a well-respected couple who owns a detective agency, Tish and Scotty are enlisted to assist Aileen and Patrick Jamieson in solving cases in Chicago while pursuing a series of unsolved murders in their own hometown as well.

Find this book on Amazon, Kindle, Nook, and Barnes & Noble Now!!

Shadowy Faces
By
Carole Walker Carter

Shadowy Faces is the second book in *the Evers and McFarlan Detective Series.* In Shadowy Faces, Tish and Scotty are confronted with the lives of three young women who have been ruined. Each young woman deals with lost weekends where all they can recall are vague faces tormenting them. These shadowy faces become the focus of the investigation of Evers and McFarlan along with the Jamiesons and the Chicago Police. The team works methodically to discover what happened to each of the women to bring the criminals to justice.

Tish needed to lean on a discipline her Grand-Master taught her even with the warning of what could happen to her if anyone should learn of her new martial arts fighting technique. Scotty also faces the threat of losing the love of his life

Find this book on Amazon, Kindle, Nook, and Barnes & Noble Now!!

Nine Points of a Circle
By
Carole Walker Carter

Carole Walker Carter

Nine Points of a Circle

Evers and McFarlan Detective Series

Nine Points of a Circle is the third book in the *Evers & McFarlan Detective Series.* In Nine Points of a Circle, Tish and Scotty are now husband and wife, owners, and licensed detectives in the Evers & McFarlan Agency. Even though the Jamison's are retired, they will continue to consult with Scotty and Tish.

Captain Jones hires the Evers and McFarlan Agency for what appears to be a serial killer. Four deaths have occurred over the past two years, and the bodies were dumped on different streets in downtown Chicago. At the same time, Tish and Scotty are approached by a well-known Chicago business executive regarding his missing daughter.

Both cases will take all of Scotty's technical expertise and Tish's detective skills to solve. Follow them as they delve into the seedy depths of the Chicago underworld.

This book will be available on Amazon, Kindle, Nook, and Barnes & Noble in the summer of 2018.

The Child Rowanda, Little Dragon
By
Carole Walker Carter

Twelve-year-old Rowanda lives with her mother in the lush garden country of Neslora. Seemingly an idyllic world with endlessly blooming flowers, buzzing bees, and birds chirping, Rowanda and her friends are confronted with the horror of the abduction of their mothers.

Rowanda finds herself confronted with the daunting task of finding and rescue her mother and the mothers of her friends. A tyrant king abducted and transported the mothers to a desert world where they are being held as slaves.

Armed only with four talismans, chosen from many by mystical means, Rowanda goes through a portal to Arolsen where her fate is intermingled with two desert dwellers. Together they join forces to brave the desert, defending themselves from nomads, terrible creatures, and scorching desert days and frigid desert nights to rescue Rowanda's mother.

The Palace City reveals the true identities of Rowanda's traveling companions and the reasons they accompanied her on her quest.

Find this book on Amazon, Kindle, Nook, and Barnes & Noble Now!!

The Child Rowanda, Return to Arolsen
By
Carole Walker Carter

When Rowanda and the Elder Sorceresses become aware that the charms left in Arolsen are causing destruction in Neslora, Rowanda, her best friend, Nalivia, as well as Beirimor, Rowanda's father and his mother, the Elder Sorceress, must return to Arolsen to set things right. Many adventures await all four of the Neslorians. Boultori, the wicked king's brother, is being held captive in the palace prison. The Neslorians plan is to rescue Boultori and place him on the throne so he can make Arolsen a safe, flourishing, and blissful world...

Rowanda finds Arolsen more fascinating as two new talismans chose Rowanda. A tiger's eye and an animal's tooth manifest their magic by controlling the most feared creatures of Arolsen. These creature's aide Rowanda on her quest for justice.

Nalivia, a new and untrained sorceress and Rowanda's childhood best friend, joins this adventure as she is tasked to find charms that will aide Boultori when he battles his evil brother, King Nashua. With help from Anarigar, a young goat herder, the two youth finds themselves in trouble.

Magic abounds in this second book of the Child Rowanda series as good battles evil to rescue a world from slavery and hardship and to keep Neslora from the same predicament.

Find this book on Amazon, Kindle, Nook, and Barnes & Noble Now!!

The Child Rowanda, Underworld

By
Carole Walker Carter

Trying to rid the world of Neslora of the evil wizard, Nashua, Rowanda finds herself dragged into the Underworld with the evil sorcerer.

Navigating the terrifying darkness of this new world, Rowanda finds a mysterious and mystical guide who reveals that Rowanda can only exit the Underworld the same way she came in, with the evil sorcerer at her side. However, Nashua must be truly repentant of his depravities before he is allowed to leave, which means Rowanda cannot leave if he does not repent.

Trying to find Nashua in the darkness and convince him to repent, becomes a difficult process. Making matters worse are the demons, intent on making both Nashua and Rowanda one of them that would mean living an eternity in the Underworld in agony.

Find this book on Amazon, Kindle, Nook, and Barnes & Noble Now!!

The Child Rowanda, Dragon Princess
By
Carole Walker Carter

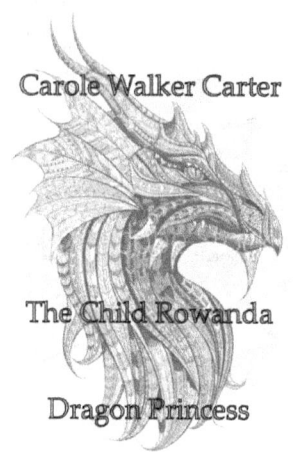

Carole Walker Carter

The Child Rowanda

Dragon Princess

Leaving the Underworld through another portal, Rowanda finds that she has not returned to her home-world of Neslora but finds herself on another parallel world with the devious Nashua, where she is elevated to a princess.

Friends and members of her family are in this world, but they are not as they should be. They are doubles with a different personality and…no recollection of Rowanda.

Rowanda finds herself at odds with her look-alike parents, the king, and queen of Soleran.

Rowanda's magical talent of charming animals allows Rowanda to help the enslaved citizens of this world by joining the rebel army in opposition to the king and queen.

Wanting nothing more than to return to her own world, Rowanda seeks the aid of a fire-breathing dragon.

Find this book on Amazon, Kindle, Nook, and Barnes & Noble Now!!

Childhood Stories my Dad Told Me
By

Carole Walker Carter

Growing up on a farm in Nebraska during the Great Depression was difficult, but for two young boys, it was also filled with fun and adventures.

These stories tell about the amusing antics that my father and his younger brother found themselves in during these hard times.

The stories are filled with insights about rural schools, country social events, and harvest time, as well as the day-to-day chores of a working farm.

Find this book on Amazon, Kindle, Nook, and Barnes & Noble Now!!

www.ingramcontent.com/pod-product-compliance
Lightning Source LLC
Chambersburg PA
CBHW070826180626
46818CB00001B/409